A Time for Faith

A Single Dad Christian Romance

Potter's House Books (Three) Book 6

By Leah J. Busboom

D1716761

Dedication

To all of you who enjoy reading faith-based romance. May this story uplift your heart.

To my amazing husband—I couldn't do this without your love and support.

Now faith is confidence in what we hope for and assurance about what we do not see. (Hebrews 11:1)

Table of Contents

Chapter One
Noah

THIS BRISK OCTOBER DAY STARTS off just like any other. The hot Colorado summer has quickly turned into autumn, the aspen trees resplendent as they dot the mountains in patches of gold. I take time for only a brief glance at God's stunning handiwork, then dash into work.

As usual, I'm one of the first people in the office. Climbing the corporate ladder has been a slow process with a couple of setbacks along the way, but I remain determined to excel. I've sacrificed my personal life for my career—I know that. But after I became a single father, I felt compelled to become a workaholic.

The open spreadsheets on my computer screen occupy my mind. I keep coming back to these numbers, even though I reported the problem to my boss, David Robertson, weeks ago. A niggle of doubt bothers me. There shouldn't be such a large discrepancy in the revenue for our latest product line. My twenty-something boss (who earned that position by being the owner's grandson) assures me that he's on top of the problem, but I'm not sure. Should I bring this issue to the attention of a higher-level executive? Can my supervisor really produce the evidence that the company isn't missing a half-million dollars in revenue even though my calculations indicate it is? Surely any executive would be grateful for my intervention, even if the discrepancy turns out to be explained away by my boss. *Right?*

It's times like this that I wish I had a colleague I trusted to turn to for advice. But I've intentionally held myself apart from relationships—personal or professional—since Victoria left. One day I was a happily married man with a new baby, the next a single dad with a fear of relationships.

Why not turn to God? The thought comes as a surprise. At one point in my life, my faith was firm and strong, but recent misfortunes made me wonder about whether He's listening to me anymore. I stifle the voice inside my head. *Noah, you can work out your problems on your own.*

The office starts to buzz as more employees arrive. I wander into the breakroom for my daily caffeine jolt. Our office manager, Mrs. Thompson, believes that coffee should resemble motor oil—black and dense enough to almost hold a spoon upright in the cup. I cut mine with some hot water, then sip slowly, letting my taste buds acclimate to the bitter flavor. *Maybe I should start bringing my own coffee. I'm sure my stomach and ulcer would thank me.* I nod to some colleagues as I walk back to my office. No one stops me for a friendly chat, just how I like it.

Several hours and a couple of cups of coffee later, Bob Robertson's executive assistant knocks on the doorjamb to my office. I put on my professional smile. Cordial enough that people don't think I dislike them, but not so amiable as to invite friendship. "How can I help you, Gladys?"

Her usually friendly expression is replaced by an uncomfortable, serious one. "Mr. Robertson would like to meet with you immediately."

My heart rate increases at her facial expression and the ominous tone of her words. She generally refers to our CEO as Bob, so why the more formal address today? Is this something to do with the discrepancy?

She lingers at the door, waiting for me to accompany her like I'm a new hire in need of direction. I grab my laptop and walk down the hall beside her. Gladys doesn't make eye contact with me, so I don't bother trying to engage her in conversation. The awkward silence between us makes me start to regret my tendency to hold people at arm's length. If I'd been friendlier with Gladys in the past, maybe she'd give me a clue as to what's about to happen. Good or bad.

Bob's office is a large corner suite overlooking the mountains—on par with what you'd expect a high-level executive to have. The view is gorgeous today, with the snow-covered Rockies against a backdrop of green grass as the lush grounds around the building start responding to the cooler autumn temperatures after the summer's drought. I've always thought the juxtaposition of the white mountains and the green valley surrounding the foothills is spectacular, but my anxiety keeps me from enjoying the view.

Gladys returns to her perch outside Bob's office as I walk inside. The business-suit clad stately gentleman is sitting at his desk. His amiable smile is missing, and a frown graces his face. He stands when I enter, motioning for me to take one of the guest chairs in front of the massive wooden desk. The plush leather chair squeaks as I slowly lower my weight into it. My left knee immediately starts bouncing in nervous anticipation of what is coming next.

"Noah, I won't beat around the bush," Bob says without preamble after he resumes his seat.

I usually enjoy his blunt style, but not today. His eyes bore into me, rendering me speechless. Where is the jolly, white-haired boss? My palms start to sweat. I swallow and nod for him to continue.

"As part of the preparation for our annual report, I commissioned an outside audit of our financials. As you know, I'd like to take the company public next year, so this was step one in that process." He clears his throat. "The auditing firm found several discrepancies in product revenue which totals around a half million dollars."

I open my mouth to speak, but he holds up his hand. "I've put David on a leave of absence until we get this mess straightened out. Unfortunately, I'm going to have to let you go. As lead financial officer, you should have found this discrepancy and brought it forward." His eyes narrow. "Unless, of course, you're the reason for it."

All my spinning thoughts and worries screech to a halt, including my bouncing knee. *Did he just say he was letting me go?*

My heart gallops in my chest and I take a deep, calming breath. Bob's lack of faith in my honesty is a real eye-opener. We've known each other for years. Surely my track record has earned his trust and respect, but I guess not. "Bob, I did find some discrepancies and identified them to David a couple weeks ago. He assured me that he was handling the situation."

I start to open my laptop, but Bob interrupts me. "Do you have any emails that you exchanged with David on this subject?"

"When I spoke to him about it, he asked me not to document my findings in any emails since he didn't know who was part of the problem." I'd thought this was odd at the time, and my better judgment told me that I should put my concerns in writing, but I never did.

"I see," Bob says in a cold voice.

"I have the spreadsheet I showed David," I say again, as I start to open the laptop sitting on my knee.

Bob extends his hand. "I'll take the laptop. Please clean your office out immediately. Security will accompany you out of the building."

"You're firing me? Just like that?" My voice rises as panic starts to overtake me.

Bob's brows draw together. "David implicated you earlier this morning. He claims you were siphoning off small amounts of money over the course of several years. Since I don't want a company scandal while we're preparing our public offering, I'm not going to press embezzlement charges at this time. But once the auditing firm untangles this mess, I will come after anyone and everyone who's taken money from this company. Am I clear?"

I stand up on shaky legs and face the man I used to respect. "Don't you think it's odd that David implicated me when I was the one who told him about the issue? Maybe he's the source of the problem."

Bob pays no attention to my last-ditch effort to save my job as he becomes engrossed in his computer screen, signaling the end of our meeting. *I guess blood is thicker than water.*

Two men wearing security shirts stand at Bob's door. They walk with me back to my desk, and I collect my meager belongings. A photo of Sofie and me. A pink pencil holder adorned with glitter that Sofie made in her kindergarten class. A mousepad with a Dilbert cartoon on it (although I don't find it particularly amusing at the moment). And an Employee of the Month plaque—I should probably just throw that in the trash can.

Tokens from my eight-year career fit comfortably in a shoebox. Once I double-check my desk drawers, finding a stray Snickers bar that I add to the box, the two men literally walk me out the door. I sit in my car in the parking lot, trying to calm my shaking hands. My mind spins, and I wonder how I'll make the next mortgage payment on my house.

Sometime later, I swipe the screen on my cell phone, realizing that I've been sitting in my car for over an hour, paralyzed and in shock. I dial and put the phone to my ear.

"Hey brother! What's up?" My younger sister answers in her usual happy-go-lucky style. Nothing ever bothers Ellie.

"I'm going to pick-up Sofie today."

She laughs. "What? My workaholic brother is leaving work early?"

"Um, something like that."

"Well, thanks. I am running a bit late today, so that saves me a trip across town."

"Good . . . Actually, I can pick Sofie up for the rest of the week." *And probably for the rest of my life.*

"Am I talking to *the* Noah Sullivan?" She teases.

A noncommittal grunt escapes. "I'll tell you more tonight, I gotta go." I quickly end the call so my sister can't ferret out why I'm suddenly available. Ellie's been a godsend since she moved in with me after my wife left—although I suspect my sister was really running away from a bad breakup. Regardless, Ellie's a great help with Sofie and has been the one to drop Sofie off in the morning and pick her up in the afternoon because my corporate job was too important for me to do menial tasks like that. *What an idiot I've been.*

I start my car and slowly drive away from the only job I've known since moving to Paradise Springs. The day I got the Robertson Industries position here was one of the happiest days of my life. *Noah Sullivan, making it big time.*

The modern concrete and glass building grows smaller and smaller in my rearview window. Since it's only an hour until I pick up Sofie, I'll find a coffee shop and grab another cup—at least it won't be like drinking sludge. I can pass the time by surfing my phone for new jobs. Why am I always starting over? First Victoria leaves me, and now I'm suddenly unemployed.

Just when I thought my life was stabilizing, it's in shambles again. First dumped by who I thought was my till-death-do-us-part wife, then discarded by what I thought was my forever company. It's no surprise that my once-unshakeable faith has vanished. *God, why have you abandoned me?*

Chapter Two
Raelynn

HAIR TOPPLES FROM THE BUN at the nape of my neck, looking like a bird's nest. I've fixed it twice already today, so now I'm just going to ignore it. A short, easy-to-care-for cut is just what I need. Maybe I can ask my fellow kindergarten teacher and friend Cassie for a hair salon recommendation. I haven't been in town long enough to find one.

I glance at the clock and breathe a sigh of relief. Parents will be arriving in fifteen minutes to pick up their kids. Frankly, I can't wait for my quiet house and a warm, satisfying meal. But those will have to wait for a little longer.

Somedays I feel like a glorified babysitter, and today is one of them. Paint spatters cover my rumpled blouse after several students became overly zealous in the finger-painting art project. And I have a sticky residue on my pants leg because Benny spilled his fruit cup on me.

Still, moving to this small town was a blessing, giving me a fresh start with my career and my personal life. I love children and have wanted to start a family for quite some time, but I haven't found that special guy yet. Maybe I'll have better prospects in this community with its strong family and Christian values.

Parental and community support in Paradise Springs has been amazing. Unlike at my previous school, parents show up for conferences with teachers, and the community goes all out to support the school in our fundraising efforts.

Principal Marshfield hired me for the full-time position just a month before school started, so I pulled up roots and moved to a place where I know no one. The move was worth it, because teaching full time is much more satisfying than being a substitute.

Lord, thank you for guiding me and giving me a new direction in my career and in my life.

A tiny hand tugs on my pantleg, drawing my eyes down. "Miss Dailey, can I put away the crayons?"

I smile at Sofie—one of my favorite and usually best-behaved students. She's always careful when she puts the crayons back in their container. "Why yes, I'd love the help."

She beams and scampers off to the activity area, her blonde curls bouncing as they spill down her back. She's a beautiful child, and she captured my heart on my first day.

I wonder about her family, because her aunt brings her and picks her up every day. The student records indicate Sofie lives with her father and there's no mother's name listed. Oddly enough, I've not met her dad even though kindergarten has been in session for over two full months already.

Parents start trickling in, waiting at the designated pickup area at the front of the room. Students squeal and rush to them, chattering a mile a minute about the finger-painting projects grasped in their tiny hands. Some parents kneel and animatedly discuss their child's painting. Others are too busy collecting their child's backpack and jacket so they can depart as quickly as possible. I watch the proceedings with interest, observing the different parenting styles.

"Daddy! Daddy!" Sofie shouts from across the room, then runs towards a tall attractive dark-haired man wearing a business suit. He beams as she smacks into his legs. A dimple appears in one of his cheeks, and my stomach does a funny little flip.

I walk over to introduce myself, extending my hand. "You must be Mr. Sullivan? I'm Miss Dailey." What bad luck to meet Sofie's dad for the first time today and have to give him a pink slip. No chance to build up some rapport with him first before hitting him with bad news.

His beaming smile fades and a polite, neutral expression crosses his face. He shakes my hand and says, "Noah Sullivan. Nice to meet you, Miss Dailey. Sofie talks about you all the time."

I smile and nod in acknowledgement, hoping to elicit another smile from him. *No such luck.* Turning to my desk, I retrieve the pink slip of paper and hand it to him. Dreading this conversation, I clear my suddenly dry throat. "Sofie, can you finish collecting the crayons for me?" Mr. Sullivan stares at the paper with a puzzled look while Sofie returns to the activity area.

Turning back to face Mr. Sullivan, I draw in a quick breath for courage. "Principal Marshfield has instructed all teachers to inform parents when there's any sort of behavioral issue in the classroom."

Sofie's dad's eyes widen, and he opens his mouth to speak. I hold up my hand, politely cutting him off. "As the paper describes, Sofie and Angela got into a little skirmish over a crayon. Apparently, it was the only turquoise one left in the box and they both wanted it. Unfortunately, Sofie pushed Angela so she could grab the crayon from the box, causing the other girl to fall to the floor. Sofie sat in timeout, giving her time to think about her actions. The two girls got along the rest of the day, but I have to report this to you."

The man I previously thought was attractive now scowls at me. No sign of that dimple. "Sofie's only five, Miss Dailey. How can a minor skirmish over a crayon cause you to write her up?" His dark eyes glare at me, pinning me in place. He's acting like I've put a blemish on his daughter's record that will stick with her until college.

"All my students are five, Mr. Sullivan." My voice sounds a little too haughty, so I tone it down. "The reason for the write-up," I nod towards the slip in his hand, "is to inform the parent and to have the parent help address the issue. A simple discussion about sharing and not shoving another student is all I'm asking you to do."

If eyes could shoot daggers, Mr. Sullivan's would be shooting them at me. "I'll *address* this with Sofie," he says in a clipped voice, forestalling any further discussion. He turns, and his face brightens again as he calls out to his daughter, "Sofie, come on, time to go home." She carefully puts away the precious crayon bucket and rejoins her dad. He takes her tiny hand, and they walk away without a backward glance.

I berate myself, wondering if I could have handled that better—used a lighter, friendlier style with the attractive Mr. Sullivan. Sometimes my no-nonsense façade puts people off. I sure got off on the wrong foot with him, and I don't know how to fix it.

Glancing around the room, I confirm that everything is in its place, then collect my overloaded book bag and leave. My quiet house isn't so appealing anymore, and I've lost my appetite. I'll stew about that interaction with Noah Sullivan for the rest of the night.

Chapter Three

Noah

SHOVING THAT DETESTABLE PINK SLIP into my pocket, I stomp to my car with Sofie in tow. A deranged laugh almost escapes at the irony of getting two pink slips in one day.

When it rains, it pours. That expression pretty much sums up my day. First, I'm fired, then my sweet Sofie is written up for an offense involving a crayon. *She's in kindergarten, for Pete's sake!* I fume when I remember Miss Dailey advising me on how to counsel my own daughter, her snotty voice strongly hinting that I didn't have a clue about how to discipline my child. Maybe I'll send Ellie in my place for the parent-teacher conference coming up next week. It would be fine by me if I never laid eyes on Miss Dailey again.

As I drive along the main thoroughfare, an idea hits me. Ellie is gone this evening, so what better time to take my daughter out to a father-daughter dinner at her favorite place? I smirk at what Miss Dailey would think about that—I'm sure she'd say I was rewarding Sofie for bad behavior.

"Want to eat at Mac and Don's?" I use our code name for the local fast-food restaurant. My eyes glance at Sofie in my rearview window as she sits in her kiddie safety seat in the back.

She perks up, clapping her tiny hands. "Is it my birthday?" she asks in an excited tone.

A stab of guilt hits me. When was the last time I took Sofie out for dinner, just her and me? Sadly, it was on her birthday last year. "No, it's not your birthday," I reply with an embarrassed chuckle. "I just want to treat my little girl to dinner."

"Yay! Can I have French fries?"

"Sure," I say as we pull into the parking lot.

We've obviously beat the rush since it's only 4:30 and there's barely a handful of people in the restaurant. An elderly couple having coffee and each eating one of those fried apple pies. Two teenage boys snarfing down a stack of hamburgers. And a man in a business suit reading a newspaper, the trash from his meal still sitting on the tray beside his elbow.

"How about a kiddie meal?" I ask Sofie as we approach the teenage girl manning the cash register. She looks bored and keeps popping her gum like she wishes she were anywhere but here.

Sofie stops her bouncing beside me. "I want a meal with a hamburger. Do I get a toy?"

I address the order-taker, "What's in your kiddie meal?"

She turns and looks at the sign above her head as if that holds the answer. "Um, a small hamburger and fries, I think," she says without making eye contact.

Sensing that it's going to be a long delay to get the answer to my question, I say, "We'll have one kiddie meal, a double hamburger with cheese, large fries, and a Coke." With how badly today went, I owe myself some greasy comfort food. At least I justify my questionable nutritional choices in my head.

The girl puts our order in the register. "Do you want a small soda or chocolate milk with the kiddie meal?"

"Chocolate milk, please," Sofie practically shouts, drawing the attention of the older couple sitting in the booth in the far back. The lady exchanges a wink with me at Sofie's exuberant outburst. I feel an immediate kinship with her for not scowling at my daughter's loudness.

After paying, we stand off to the side, waiting for our food. Sofie retrieves far too many napkins from the dispenser, but I don't say anything. I can always put them in the glove compartment in the car for use another day.

"Number 241!" the girl who took our order yells from her place behind the counter. Since there's no one else waiting for food, I find it amusing that she couldn't just hand me the tray. Mentally shrugging, I grab the tray and let Sofie pick a booth, where we settle in with our food.

Sofie swings her short legs (which don't come close to touching the ground) and chatters the entire meal. Her animated discussion keeps my mind from drifting to my woes. She shows me the plastic toy, which luckily was included in the meal. I can't tell what animal the lime green figure is supposed to be, but at least Sofie's happy with it.

I learn about finger painting and how fun it is to put your fingers directly into the paint. My daughter extols Miss Dailey's many good qualities, such as her ability to act out a storybook—doing a mean rendition of a donkey named Fred. Miss Dailey can peel an orange so the peel comes off in one long spiral, and she can keep some naughty boy named Oliver from throwing mud on everyone in the playground. According to my daughter, Miss Dailey is a saint with a heart of gold. *Maybe my bad first impression of Miss Dailey was a bit rash.*

Once we're back in the car, my double hamburger and fries sit like a rock in my stomach. I generally don't eat fast food, so my body is probably having a difficult time processing it. Or is it that I'm not as young as I used to be? I'll hit up the Tums once I get home.

"Daddy, can I watch *Frozen* when we get home?"

A groan nearly escapes, but I manage to suppress it. This will be our hundredth viewing of the animated feature. I hate to admit it, but I can sing *Let It Go* with the best of them. "Sure, honey," I say reluctantly.

As we walk inside my fancy, 4000-square-foot house, my financial worries hit me like a slap in the face. Viewing the movie is a brilliant idea. It'll keep my mind off my current lack of employment, and I can forget about Miss Dailey's reprimand and that onerous write-up slip in my pocket. I really should take Elsa's advice. *Let. It. Go.* At least for tonight.

Chapter Four

Raelynn

I DIDN'T ANTICIPATE HOW LONG it would take to make friends in this small town. After leaving all my friends and family behind in Denver, I figured I could easily meet my new neighbors, my new colleagues, and even people at the grocery store. The thing is, everyone may know everyone in Paradise Springs, but an outsider isn't readily accepted in their tight-knit clique. I'm known as "that lady from the big city."

Mom always told me that the best place to meet people is at church, so I've been attending the FaithBridge Church on Third Street for a couple weeks now. I was drawn to the beautiful brick exterior, stained-glass windows, and the tall, majestic steeple. Plus, the sign out front said, "Everyone Welcome."

The first Sunday, I decided to attend the nine o'clock service, which I thought might be a little more sparsely attended. Apparently, there's reserved seating for that service because several people asked me to move because I was "in their seat." Once I found a spot in the unreserved section in the back pew, everything went well.

I enjoyed Pastor Tim's sermon about forgiveness. He recounted the story from Genesis about Joseph. I'm always amazed how the story of forgiveness culminates when Joseph reveals himself and forgives his brothers for selling him into slavery. I was moved by Pastor Tim's words and wondered if someone did a terrible thing to me, could I be like Joseph and forgive them?

Today when I arrive, I immediately take the same seat as I have every time since that awkward first time. No one asks me to move, so maybe I've found what can now always be *my seat*. The choir sings several uplifting songs. Pastor Tim talks about not judging others. I think back to my conversation with Noah Sullivan and recognize that I may have been judgmental in my little speech about how he should handle the situation with Sofie. Since he never appeared until months into the school year, I assumed he was an uninvolved parent, and that may have colored my view of him and how I handled the write-up slip. I vow to apologize to Mr. Sullivan next time I see him.

God, please help me to not judge others, as I would want them not to judge me.

As the service wraps up, Pastor Tim points to the huge stained-glass window adorning the rear wall in the church. "Our century-old window is in dire need of repair." As he says the words, I notice some cracking and discoloration that aren't noticeable unless you look closely. "We got a bid from a restoration company, but it would cost us $25,000 to have them do the work." Gasps echo around the room at the exorbitant price. "I have faith that God will help us find a solution." He grins, looking across the audience. "If anyone knows anyone with stained-glass experience, please talk to me after the service. We can use all the help we can get."

I remain in the pew for a few minutes, stunned at the timely plea for help. *Is this finally my chance to make new friends?* God works in mysterious ways, because I've done stained glass for over ten years, even restoring a few smaller windows in older homes in my former neighborhood. My experience may not be enough to restore the enormous window by myself, but I'm willing to assist. My heart lifts, knowing that I can help this congregation and that this will give me an opportunity to meet some new people in the process. I eagerly approach Pastor Tim and volunteer.

~*~

The next Tuesday, Pastor Tim calls to say that he's found another person willing to help with the stained-glass restoration project. He wants to meet with us this evening. I tell him that I can meet after work, so we agree on five o'clock.

When I pull into the church parking lot, there's only two other cars. I walk into the church and spot Pastor Tim talking to another man. They're both examining the massive window with their backs to me. As I walk towards them, I notice how the other man towers over the pastor by several inches. He's tall and fit, his dark hair curling slightly at his collar. Since my footsteps are muffled by the carpeted walkway, they don't hear me. I clear my throat once I'm standing a few feet away.

Both men turn, and my heart sinks like a rock. Noah Sullivan is the man standing next to Pastor Tim.

"Raelynn, so nice to see you again," Pastor Tim says in his cheery voice. A bright smile lights up his face as if I'm a long-lost cousin. "Let me introduce you to Noah Sullivan. He's also volunteered to help restore our stained-glass window."

Noah and I stare awkwardly at each other for several beats. A pin could drop and be clearly heard in the dead silence hanging between us. I finally come to my senses, and good manners take over. I smile and say in an overly friendly voice, "Noah and I've met. His daughter is in my kindergarten class."

Noah nods with a slight frown on his face, while Pastor Tim beams, looking at both of us like a proud father. "Even better!" the pastor says. "I'd love to stay, but the missus is expecting me home for dinner. I'll leave you two to discuss the window. Just let me know how I can help, and give me a heads up when you need access to the sanctuary. Bye!" He strides down the aisle and is gone in the blink of an eye.

I turn back to Noah, regretting that I volunteered for this project and internally debating how to gracefully get out of this.

The drawn expression on Noah's face tells me he's probably thinking the same thing.

"Here's the ladder you requested." Noah and I both jump as an older gentleman appears, hefting a long ladder up beside the window. I gulp at how high the ladder reaches. My fear of heights kicks in. *Boy, I sure didn't think this project through, did I?*

"Thanks," Noah says. The guy nods and returns to the front of the church and out of sight. After a long pause, Noah turns to me. "I thought we could identify all the areas that need work and then discuss how best to fix them. Although I have some experience with stained-glass restoration, we might need to get some advice from an expert." Noah raises an eyebrow, "Unless you're an expert?" His skeptical expression tells me that he doubts my expertise.

"Um, well, I've helped restore a few windows in the historical district in my old neighborhood. But this project is much more massive than any I've undertaken before."

Noah shakes his head in agreement. "I repaired a few of the church windows near the entry last year," he nods his chin towards the two beautiful windows near the front entrance. "My sister's boss goes to this church, and she mentioned to Ellie that they needed volunteers. Ellie knew how much I used to enjoy working with stained-glass, and one thing led to another . . ." He trails off with an embarrassed shrug. "That's why Pastor Tim asked for my help again with this project, but I've never tackled anything this large before either."

Ah, so Mr. Sullivan wasn't exactly a volunteer. I suspect that no one can turn down Pastor Tim when he asks for your help.

Now's the time to address the elephant in the room and get it out of the way before we go any further. "Let me ask this first, do you even want to work with me?"

My bluntness takes him by surprise. His eyes widen and he blinks at me several times before he responds. "Why wouldn't I want to work with you?"

I shift nervously back and forth on my feet. "Mr. Sullivan, I was rude and judgmental when we talked in my classroom. I apologize for that, but I'll also understand if you don't want to work with me."

His lips twitch into the semblance of a small smile. "Let's start over." He extends his hand. "I'm Noah Sullivan. Please call me Noah."

I blush like an adolescent girl at his flirty smile. Extending my hand to shake his, I feel a tingle zip up my arm. "I'm Raelynn, but all my friends call me Rae." We smile pleasantly at each other for a few seconds.

Noah pulls out of our staring match and points to the ladder sitting beside the window. "Do you want to examine the window first or should I?"

"How about I take notes and you do the climbing?" I pull my laptop out of my purse and take a seat in the nearby pew, leaving no room for debate as to who's climbing that ladder. *No need to admit to my fear of heights.*

With a shrug, Noah scales the tall ladder. I notice his toned muscles and how easy he makes it look to climb to that height. *Gulp.*

He pauses beside the first one of the cracked pieces. Pulling a tape measure out of his pocket, he measures the crack. "Six-inch crack in the yellow glass that makes up the top left corner of the manger."

I pull out a pad of graph paper and make a quick drawing of the window, which is made up of a series of four sections, each section enclosed in a wooden frame. The very traditional scene depicts the baby Jesus in the manger, with Mary and Joseph flanking the child. Two shepherds and a sheep stand off to one side, while the three wise men stand off to the other.

I chuckle as I sketch, remembering an article I read about a church in Steamboat Springs that has a stained-glass window portraying Jesus on skis. Because this window was originally constructed 100 years ago, it probably didn't occur to the designer to create anything too unconventional.

Since I'm using grid paper, I number the grids so we can reference each piece of glass easily. Noah watches me from his perch on the ladder. "That's a great idea, Rae. And you're quite an artist."

Looking up from my drawing, I smile. "I also have an art degree, but these days all I get to use it for is finger painting or paper-mache."

He laughs. "Well then, let's hope this project makes better use of that skill."

Noah climbs higher, stopping to describe each flaw in the glass. He identifies cracks, discolored glass, as well as areas where the lead between sections has decayed. In places where the lead joints are very deteriorated, Noah taps lightly on the glass to see if moves or rattles. I note when a section rattles, indicating that the integrity of that part of the window is compromised by the deterioration.

Noah descends and moves the ladder over, then repeats the process in the next section and the next section. It's a tedious process and takes about an hour, but eventually we identify all the areas that need repair. It's quite overwhelming how much of the window needs restoration.

Noah takes a breather and sits beside me as I enter the last of the information. His dark eyes look at me intently, tracking my every movement. "The details on your drawing and how you've labeled everything is extraordinary."

A warm blush heats my cheeks at his unexpected compliment. "I used this technique for the smaller windows I restored in my former neighborhood, and it was extremely helpful. I'll scan in the picture and email it to you, along with the spreadsheet."

As we turn to walk out, Noah says, "I also need to apologize for my behavior when we first met. I wasn't having a particularly good day, and I took it out on you."

I wave my hand. "Please, let's forget all about that. We both made mistakes that day."

He nods, accepting my suggestion. "Once we've digested the spreadsheet, do you want to meet so we can give Pastor Tim a proposal and timeline for the work?"

I stop and pull out my cell phone. "Sure, what day works best for you, and what time?"

He replies with a nervous chuckle. "We can work around your schedule, Rae."

Giving him a puzzled look, I wonder why his schedule is suddenly so flexible when he couldn't be bothered to bring his daughter to school or pick her up until a week ago. I mentally smack myself. *Here I go again with my judgmental thoughts.* "How about Friday at two? Kindergarten gets off at noon that day. We can meet here or at a coffee shop."

He nods. "Let's meet at the Sacred Grounds coffee shop."

I suppress a giggle—the name sure seems fitting, considering our project. I agree and email him a calendar invite.

"You can bring Sofie along if you need to," I add.

Noah smiles. "My sister can watch her. I think we need to focus on the plan without interruption from a five-year-old."

I laugh. "True."

We leave the church and walk to our respective cars. I have a spring in my step and a lightness in my heart. Is it because of the satisfaction of serving the church or because of the handsome man helping me? *Maybe a little of both.*

Chapter Five
Noah

SOME DAYS I PANIC WHEN I see a police car drive down my street, terrified that they're here to arrest me. I'm just waiting for the other shoe to drop and for Mr. Robertson to press charges against me.

Although I know I'm innocent, David may have been able to "cook the books" and make it look like I was the one embezzling the money. I feel helpless to do anything further since Mr. Robertson made it clear that blood is thicker than water when he "let me go."

My blood still boils that he wouldn't even allow me to show him the spreadsheet where I had found the discrepancy. Since Robertson Industries seized the laptop, I have no way to do any more research. I'll just keep my lawyer on speed dial in case something develops.

After having a lot of time to ponder the situation, I'm convinced that David is the culprit. Whether he will ever be caught is another matter. *Will I ever get closure?*

I'd forgotten how tedious and confidence-destroying looking for a new job is. Longing to get my old life back—or at least the salary I once enjoyed—I enrolled in all the traditional job sites that post high-paying, corporate job opportunities, but there's very few finance positions available in this area. If I want to commute to Denver every day, I have a lot to choose from. Driving over an hour each way is a hard pass for me, especially with Sofie to consider.

Now that my schedule is more flexible (let's be honest, it's wide-open every day), I take Sofie to school and pick her up afterwards. Ellie deserves a break. Her job at the used furniture store, Twice Again, doesn't start until 9 o'clock, which gave her plenty of time for drop-off. It also allowed Ellie time to pick up Sofie in the afternoon because she could combine child pickup with an errand for the store. So, I focused on my job and let Ellie do child transportation duty.

The thing is, since being fired, I've loved getting to spend time with my daughter. I didn't know what I was missing. When we drive to school, I hear Sofie talk excitedly about what Miss Dailey has planned for them and then at the end of the day I hear about how those activities went. Billy spilled milk on the story time rug. Angela hogged all the pretty crayons (this is a reoccurring theme). Liam got a bloody nose. Emma tripped and knocked over an easel, breaking off the leg. The minor catastrophes go on and on. I've come to appreciate Miss Dailey and agree that she must be a saint with a heart of gold.

Unfortunately, the urgency to get another job increases every day because of the house. The term "house rich, cash poor" perfectly describes my situation. When I purchased the four-bedroom, craftsman-style home, I knew the monthly mortgage payment would be a stretch. Then as I continued to move up the ladder at Robertson Industries, money became the driving motivator, turning me into a workaholic. But unfortunately, as my salary increased, so did my spending.

I bought a fancy SUV . . . A 75-inch TV . . . Hired a high-end construction company to remodel the kitchen. My debt piled up, but I was still able to make the monthly payments, and I never even considered that none of my salary was going towards savings. I just kept digging myself a deeper and deeper financial hole. Now all these possessions are like a heavy stone around my neck. Next month, I won't be able to make the mortgage payments any longer.

My financial situation fuels my anger towards Robertson Industries, even though I'm trying to turn those negative thoughts into positive motivation.

Like a light bulb going on, a solution hits me. Feeling better for the first time in weeks, I walk into the kitchen where Ellie's quietly sipping coffee and preparing for her day. I grin when I notice her long brown hair piled haphazardly on her head in a messy bun. *Guess she's not quite ready for her day.*

With Sofie already dropped off at school, I have a little time to discuss my newly formed plan with my sister. Pouring myself a mug of perfectly brewed coffee, I sit across from Ellie. "I'm going to put the house on the market."

She looks up from her cell phone, her brown eyes wide with surprise. "Is the financial situation that bad, Noah?"

I grimace in embarrassment at what I'm about to admit to my sister. "Unfortunately, it is. Next month I won't be able to make the mortgage payment."

"I can start paying rent—"

I hold up a hand to stop her. "That isn't what I meant. This house is no longer affordable. We can downsize and still be comfortable. Who needs four bedrooms, four bathrooms, a great room, a living room, an office nook, and a butler's pantry?"

We exchange grins as I rattle off a list of all the house's amenities—perfect for a large family but features we don't need.

"When you put it like that, I guess you can downsize. Margaret offered me the apartment over the store, and I think it would be a great option for me."

My brows draw together in concern. "I don't mean you have to move out; we can find something that fits all of us."

Ellie smiles. "Noah, you don't need me anymore. Sofie's growing up. I'll still be in town and can babysit and help. Living above the store gives me a lot more time to work on refinishing all the furniture that Margaret finds at estate sales. I love doing that!"

Her easy acceptance of a new living situation warms my heart. I wouldn't want her to think I evicted her or that I don't want her help anymore. "How did I get so lucky to have a sister like you?"

She shrugs and goes back to sipping her coffee.

I feel like a heavy burden has been lifted from my shoulders. I put a reminder in my phone to look up my next-door neighbor's real estate agent. That seemed to be a quick, easy sale, and the neighbor was very satisfied.

~*~

The Sacred Grounds is surprisingly busy for a Friday afternoon. Looking around the cozy café, I see Rae sitting in a booth near the windows. She waves at me, and I meander around the tables scattered throughout the room to join her. Since we agreed last time to put our rocky first encounter at Sofie's school behind us, I've been looking forward to this meetup all week. *Am I attracted to the kindergarten teacher?*

"I already ordered." She nods towards the carafe sitting between us. "Is decaf alright? I don't need caffeine this time of day."

"Sounds good," I say as I pour some coffee into the extra mug beside the carafe. Rae has her laptop open and the window sketch lying on the table.

"I'm so impressed with your spreadsheet," I say between sips. The coffee has a delicious nutty flavor that I haven't tried before.

A pink blush stains her cheeks. "Thank you."

"That said, the number of repairs is rather overwhelming when you look at the list." Rae nods her agreement. "My experience is that we'll have to remove each section and lay it flat for the restoration work. That means we'll have to cover that section so wind and rain don't get in while we do the work."

She taps a finger on her enticing red lips. "The sections are quite large; are you worried about how we remove them so we don't cause more damage?"

Rae just vocalized my exact worries. "Yeah, I'm definitely worried about that. I wonder if we should hire a restoration company to remove the sections. We might be able to handle restoring and repairing each section ourselves, but some additional expertise on this project sure would help."

I chuckle internally as Rae avidly takes notes on her laptop. She's one organized woman.

Looking up at me she says, "How much do you think just the window removal will cost? From what Pastor Tim said, sounds like restoration companies charge high rates."

Drumming my fingers on the tabletop, I ponder how we solve the financial problem. "Do you think Pastor Tim would be willing to do a fundraiser? I'm just not confident that you or I can get those windows down without damaging them further."

We gaze at each other for a few seconds, each thinking about the money dilemma. With my current financial situation, I can relate to having a tight budget.

Rae shrugs. "Let's talk to Pastor Tim and get his ideas for how to raise money. Do you know any restoration companies we could approach? Maybe they would be willing to donate some of their time."

I snap my fingers. "Actually, I do know someone! I met with him when I restored the windows by the entry. Frank's a grumpy old guy, but very experienced. Would you be willing to go with me to meet with him?" *Hope he's still in business (and still alive).*

A shy smile crosses Rae's face. "Of course. Maybe between the two of us we can persuade him."

I bark out a laugh. "I think you have a better chance than me." She joins me in laughter.

We finish our coffee, and I feel confident in our start of a plan.

"Noah, may I ask why you're doing this? Are you a member of the congregation?"

My eyes don't quite meet hers. *I've asked myself the same question.* "No, I'm not a member."

She nods, and her eyes encourage me to expound further.

"I love working with stained glass," I say, not intending to explain myself any further. But Rae stares at me with such a supportive, open expression, my tongue is suddenly loosened. "When I was in college, I worked part-time for a stained-glass restoration company in Denver. During that stint, I helped with several small church window projects."

"Why didn't you continue doing restoration if you like it so much?"

How do I explain that life got in the way? I got married, took the high-paying job, focused on climbing the corporate ladder, and never looked back. "My job at Robertson Industries was too time consuming. But the truth is, I have a lot of time on my hands right now." *Why did I blurt out that little tidbit?*

"Oh, how so?"

I shift on the suddenly hard bench seat. "Well, I was fired about a month ago." I cringe at my honesty but am relieved I don't have to dance around this issue any longer.

Rae's mouth drops open. "So that's why you drop off and pick up Sofie now," she says in a low voice, as if she's talking to herself. "Noah, I'm really sorry. I didn't know you were going through a rough patch."

I shrug. "There's still hope I'll find something, but jobs that I qualify for are few and far between here in Paradise Springs."

She reaches across the table and squeezes my hand. "Have you considered starting your own business?"

Her suggestion takes me by surprise because of how obvious it is. "No, I haven't thought that far ahead yet."

"Well, if you need someone to talk to, I'm here . . . I trust that God will show you the way."

Her eyes brighten as she says the words, and her confidence in her faith instantly makes me feel better. I squeeze her hand back. Maybe she's right. *Maybe God hasn't abandoned me. I just haven't been listening.*

Clearing my throat, I say, "I'll get that meeting set up with the restoration guy. Does Saturday work for you? He lives about an hour away."

"Yes, that's perfect." Rae collects her stuff and stands to leave.

"Thank you for the words of encouragement," I say as we walk out of the café together. I'm surprised how quickly I opened my heart to friendship again. Rae seems like just the kind of friend I need in my life right now.

Chapter Six

Raelynn

NOAH'S SITUATION MAKES ME PONDER my own life. If I lost my job, would I be able to survive for long financially? Fortunately, I put down a large down payment on my little two-bedroom bungalow between the money I saved from teaching and a modest inheritance from my grandmother. Since my mortgage payments aren't outrageous, I'd be okay for a while, but I wouldn't be able to replace my ten-year-old sedan next year like I planned. *Maybe I should start saving more.*

I've been keeping Noah in my prayers and asking God to guide him through this difficult time. I'm encouraged that, as we work together, we'll become friends. *Could we even be more than friends?* I bat that thought away as quick as it comes. Even though I yearn to start a family and Noah seems to have the same values I do, the "no dating" policy between teachers and parents that Principal Marshfield reviewed with me my first day on the job concerns me. I definitely can't date Noah without violating that policy. But does a strong friendship violate the rules?

Saturday arrives for the outing with Noah, and I take special care in my appearance. I know it's silly because he hasn't hinted at anything other than working together on the stained-glass project. I'm the one foolishly hoping to form a friendship with him. So, I mess with my hair for the fourth time and consider changing shirts twice before he gets here. *Would I look better in red?*

Ding Dong!

I cringe. *Too late, can't change my outfit now.*

Noah's standing at the door in a pair of faded blue jeans and a black long-sleeve T-shirt that he fills out very nicely. He looks like the cute boy next door sporting a bad-boy outfit. Butterflies erupt in my stomach just at the sight of him. I take a fortifying breath and open the door wider.

"Ready?" Noah asks politely as he peeks over my shoulder, looking around my tiny living room for a few beats. His eyes swivel back to me. "Did you paint that picture?"

I turn towards the bright, colorful painting hanging on the far wall in the small room. "Actually, I did. Want a closer look?"

He nods and we walk over to the painting. It's a scene featuring the river in Paradise Springs when the water rushes over the rocks during the spring thaw from the mountains. The brilliant blue, green, gray, and white tones portray God's stunning creation. Noah clears his throat. "That's amazing, Rae. You captured the movement of the water perfectly." He turns more fully to me. "You're extremely talented."

A blush floods my cheeks. "It's a fun hobby."

He raises an eyebrow. "You could sell these."

I laugh. "Thank you, but it's still a hobby." Quickly changing the subject, I point towards the kitchen, "Should I bring any bottled water?"

Noah laughs. "I brought a small cooler with water and some snacks."

I smile. "Great minds think alike, I guess." I grab a jacket since our November weather can be rather unpredictable. *Come to think of it, Colorado weather can always be unpredictable.*

Once we're in his huge SUV, I notice all the fancy gadgets, leather seats, and luxurious interior. It makes my little sedan look like a dump. "Wow, this is a really nice vehicle," I say as I sink into the plush seat.

He grunts. "I'm probably going to have to sell it. If the house sells quickly, I might be able to keep the car."

I let out a small gasp. "You're selling your house?" His financial situation must really be dire.

"Yep. Put it on the market this week and we've already had two showings. It's much bigger than I really need, and I can't afford it any longer."

My heart sinks for him and Sofie. "Where will you go?"

He shrugs. "We'll cross that bridge when we get there."

Laughing, I say, "My mom used to say that all the time."

He gives me one of his knee-weakening smiles. "Mine too."

We listen to the radio in companionable silence for several miles. When Noah turns off the main highway to a smaller secondary road, he says, "Frank lives out in the boonies. I hope I remember how to get there because the GPS won't be able to help us."

"I hope so too!" I would have worn different shoes if I thought I'd have to hoof it for any distance.

Noah clears his throat. "Don't be put off by Frank. He's kind of crotchety."

"Does that mean he's an old coot with no manners?" I tease.

"Pretty much."

The SUV bonces on the rutted dirt road and silence falls between us again because the jarring makes it impossible to talk. After a few miles, a rundown house and a dilapidated barn come into view. Noah parks outside the house and we get out. The screen door makes a loud *squeeeak* as a white-haired man in shabby overalls shuffles out onto the porch.

"Hello, Frank! We talked on the phone about a stained-glass restoration project in Paradise Springs."

The man grunts. "Come on inside."

We follow him into the house that smells like dust and pets. My nose crinkles and I try not to sneeze. Frank sits in a battered recliner while Noah and I take seats on the couch.

"I'm Noah and this is Raelynn."

Frank squints at us. "You two married?"

I only barely keep my jaw from dropping open. "No, we're just working on this project together," I rush to explain our relationship.

"I'd say you're a lucky man, Noah. Having a pretty lady like this to work on the project with you."

Noah gives me an embarrassed smile. "True," he says while I blush and remain silent at the somewhat chauvinistic remark.

After a few awkward beats, Noah leans forward towards Frank. "We want to discuss dismantling the large window in the FaithBridge Church since Rae and I are going to be restoring each section."

Frank nods his head. "I remember that big window from when we did the little ones up front. That one's going to be a bear."

My heart sinks at his discouraging words.

"Can you help us dismantle it or give us the name of someone who can?" Noah asks.

Frank looks thoughtful for a few seconds. He rests his stubble-covered chin in his hands as he thinks. "Mary would want me to help out. Being it's the Christian thing to do."

Noah and I exchange puzzled looks.

Frank laughs. "I wasn't referring to the Mother Mary." He laughs for a few more seconds, then says, "Mary was my wife. Married forty-two years. I lost her in December, two years ago."

I blink back tears. "I'm sorry for your loss." Noah echoes the sentiment.

Frank waves his hand, dismissing our condolences. "I know I'll see her again when it's my turn to go," he says matter-of-factly. He repositions the recliner to a more upright position. "Now, when can I help remove those sections?"

After a lengthy discussion about removing each section, restoring it, and putting it back, we work out a skeleton schedule. Noah smirks at me as I enter the dates on my cell phone calendar and if Frank weren't here, I'd stick my tongue out at Noah's teasing. We agree to tackle the first section next Saturday afternoon. That gives Noah and me enough time to get the supplies for the actual restoring.

We all shake hands and Frank even waves to us as we drive out of sight. Once we're back on the smooth pavement, Noah asks, "What did you think of Frank?"

"I like him. He's a little crusty on the outside, but good-hearted on the inside."

Noah laughs. "I guess that pretty much describes him."

"At least he's going to help us for no charge."

Noah nods. "True. The one thing I'll say about a church project is you find that most people are willing to help for free."

The truth in his words hit me. When I was twelve, my dad passed away. The church ladies were the first ones to bring food to our house. We had enough food to last a month. Mom was so grateful, since she was drowning in grief at the time and didn't feel like doing anything, much less cook. The meals were a godsend.

"Would you like to stop for a bite to eat on the way home?" Noah's question breaks through my thoughts.

At the mention of food, my stomach does an inelegant growl that reverberates inside the car.

"I guess that's a yes?" He chuckles.

An embarrassed laugh escapes my lips. "Sure, where do you want to go?"

"Jose's Tacos makes a mean quesadilla," Noah says.

"I love that place!"

Noah smiles. "Tacos it is."

~*~

Jose's is packed when we arrive. The place is always popular, but especially on a Saturday night. We place our order up front and find a small table in the corner. Conversations buzz around us, and a waiter brings two ice waters, a diet Pepsi for me, and Noah's beer.

"How long have you lived in Paradise Springs?" Noah asks as he sips his beer.

"I moved here a month before school started when a full-time teaching position suddenly opened up." The ice-cold soda looks refreshing, so I take a long sip enjoying the way that it tickles my taste buds. My nose wrinkles from the carbonated bubbles.

Noah chuckles. "You look just like Sofie when she drinks soda."

Not sure whether that's a compliment or not, I smile and nod.

"Where did you move here from?"

Noah's doing all the heavy lifting in this conversation, so I need to keep my end of it up a little better. "I moved from Denver. The teaching position I had there was a substitute one. I really wanted my own class where I can get to know the students and parents better."

"Do you like it so far?"

I nod my head vigorously. "Yes, I love it so much. All the kids are terrific, and the parents are very supportive, unlike my previous school."

Noah grins at the irony of my words considering my first impression of *him*. "You mean most aren't like me?" he teases. I blush, and thankfully he changes the topic. "How about Paradise Springs. Do you like living in a small town?"

I brighten at this topic. "The small-town feel is great. No traffic. Lots of interesting shops. But I've had a little trouble meeting people. Aside from my fellow teachers, and my students and their parents, I haven't built up a large circle of friends yet. That's why I joined the church."

A thoughtful expression crosses his handsome face. "You know my sister Ellie from her dropping off and picking up Sofie, right?"

"Oh, yes. She's genuinely nice. But I don't know her well since she's always just popping in and out." I bite my tongue realizing those words could be interpreted as criticism. Noah doesn't seem to notice.

"You two would get along well. I'll introduce you outside school drop-offs."

I smile, relieved that I didn't unintentionally offend him. "That would be great."

The waiter interrupts our conversation by delivering the entrees. Once he leaves, Noah continues. "I hate to admit it, but I was so busy working and trying to climb the corporate ladder, I haven't made many friends here either."

My brows draw together. "How long have you lived here?"

An embarrassed look crosses Noah's face. "Eight years."

Wow. That takes me by surprise, and I don't hide my puzzlement very well.

"I know that sounds like a long time. But one thing led to another. When Sofie's mom left, it was a difficult time—adjusting to raising a newborn by myself. When Sofie got older, there was daycare to worry about, although my sister eventually moved in to help me out. Then my job responsibilities increased . . ." His voice trails off and he shrugs apologetically.

I want to delve into why Sofie's mom left, but I don't feel like I know Noah well enough yet to do so. Maybe he'll tell me in his own time. "That's a lot to handle," I say with a sympathetic look.

An awkward silence falls between us. After a few bites, I point to my Mama Rosa's Quesadilla Plate and say, "These are delicious. They really hit the spot."

Noah nods. "The sopaipillas are also delicious, if you want to get a couple at the end of the meal."

I grin. "I'm in. Sugar's always popular with me."

We end up talking about our favorite Mexican foods and the best Mexican restaurants in Denver. Noah takes me home and I thank him for dinner. After he's gone, I realize that this is the first "date" I've gone on since I moved to Paradise Springs. My heart sinks, knowing that despite my attraction to the handsome single dad, I can't start a relationship with Noah because he's the parent of one of my students. Sadly, we can only be friends.

Chapter Seven

Noah

I'M STILL ADJUSTING TO MONDAYS. When I first wake up, I think I need to immediately tumble out of bed, put on a suit, and get ready to go to work. Then it hits me—I have no job to go to. For some reason, my unemployed status impacts me hardest on Mondays.

As strange as it sounds, I miss those early mornings in the office sipping on too-strong coffee and working on a challenging spreadsheet until all the numbers balance perfectly. I quickly steer my thoughts in another direction, knowing that the one time the numbers didn't balance caused me to lose my job. Anger, frustration, and worry over that debacle still rankle, but I'm trying to put it behind me.

As I'm leisurely sipping coffee after dropping Sofie off and waving to a busy, distracted Rae, the ringtone of my real estate agent peals through my cell phone.

"Charlie, you're calling early."

He chuckles. "I have great news! We received an offer on your house. Do you have time to review it this morning?"

My heart stops. *An offer so soon? Where are we going to live?* Mentally calming myself, I say, "Yes, I have time this morning. When should we meet?"

"I'll stop by around ten so we can talk in person. I can go over all the details of the contract." I hear papers shuffling, and he continues, "It's a strong offer, Noah."

He signs off and my mind spins. Selling the house is what needs to happen, but am I ready to give up the only home Sofie's ever known?

Not more than five minutes later, a yawning Ellie waltzes in, needing caffeine as much as I do. She pours a mug of coffee and joins me at the table.

"I have a business idea for you," she says before I have a chance to tell her about the offer on the house.

"Oh? What is it?" Ellie's ideas usually range from crazy to crazier.

"Margaret mentioned to me how stressed out she is with the Twice Again finances. She tried using QuickBooks on her own but didn't have time to keep up with it. She asked me if she could hire you to keep her books, make sure invoices go out on time, do her taxes—stuff like that. Sounds like she'll pay whatever price you want because she's desperate for help."

I sip my coffee mulling over Ellie's suggestion. *Start my own business. . .* That's the second time this idea has come up, and it's growing on me. My expertise could help many small businesses with their finances. *I don't know why I didn't seriously consider this sooner.*

There's plenty of small shops like Twice Again, and several service companies, in this town, so I should be able to make a decent salary—albeit not as much as I was making at Robertson Industries. Plus, running my own business would allow me more flexible hours and I could work from home.

"Ellie, that's a terrific idea. Give me Margaret's number and I'll get in touch with her to kick around some ideas." I grin as my heart lifts with excitement over this new venture. "I need to put together a business plan!"

My sister smiles at my enthusiasm. "You'll blow Margaret away with your expertise. Can you call her today?"

"Sure." My Monday calendar is suddenly filling up. *God works in mysterious ways.* My faith that He will guide me out of this rough patch grows by the minute.

Ellie texts over Margaret's number as I refill my mug. "Call her right away."

"I will. Oh, and I got an offer on the house. I'm meeting at ten with Charlie to discuss it."

Ellie's eyes go big as saucers. "That was fast. I guess the old saying is true. When it rains, it pours."

We both laugh. This time it's a most welcome rain.

~*~

Margaret insists that we meet this afternoon, so I add her to my suddenly packed schedule. When I arrive at Twice Again, Ellie's boss greets me like she's known me for years, although we've previously only been introduced in passing.

"Noah! You've come to save the day! Let's go back in my office to talk." The surprisingly spry seventy-year-old ushers me towards the back of the store while Ellie gives me a thumbs up from her place behind the sales counter.

After declining coffee and a donut, I settle into a chair beside Margaret's desk and say in an apologetic tone, "I don't have a formal business plan or pricing structure yet . . ."

Margaret jumps in before I can explain further. "Do you know how to use QuickBooks and do those computer sheets?"

I grin at her enthusiasm. "Yes, I know QuickBooks and spreadsheets . . ."

"Sold! When can you start?" She claps her hands as if this is the end of the discussion.

A laugh escapes. "Really? You don't need to see my credentials or what my services cost?" My voice sounds almost disappointed that I don't need to give her more of a sales pitch and that signing her up for my services is going to be a slam dunk.

The gray-haired lady leans forward in her chair as if she's going to impart confidential information. "You're the answer to my prayers, Noah. I stink at this computer stuff," she says with a wry grin.

Trying to regroup at the speed my new business is apparently blasting off, I say, "How about I put together a contract, you review it, and then if you're happy with it you can sign it and we'll get started."

She hops to her feet. "The sooner the better! Now, how about that cup of coffee? Do you take cream or sugar?"

By the time I leave the store, I've consumed two cups of coffee and a rather stale donut—not that I'd ever tell sweet Margaret that. While we shared coffee, Margaret rattled off several other of her business friends who need my help. Shaking my head in bemusement, I grin at how the septuagenarian bowled me over like a speeding train. There's no stopping Margaret once she gets going, that's for sure. *Can my brand-new business take off as fast?*

~*~

I sink down on the couch, exhausted after my busy day. It's like my life went from moving at a snail's pace to moving at warp speed. I can't keep up. My fingers itch to text Rae and share all my news. She's quickly becoming a special friend. When I pick up Sofie, maybe there'll be a little time to chat with her.

The offer on the house was as good as Charlie indicated. I didn't even submit a counter to any of their terms. The offer is signed, and if all goes well, the new buyers take possession in thirty days. I can hear a clock ticking in my head, counting down the days, and it's a little overwhelming. Charlie assured me he'll put me in contact with a reliable handyman to make a few repairs that the buyers asked for.

After meeting with Margret, I have leads for eight more business owners who may need my help. The kind-hearted lady said she'd call all of them and tell them to expect a call from me. With her on my side, I'm not going to need to do any marketing for my new business.

How did I go from despair to euphoria? My brain is suffering whiplash from the sudden change of fortune. I belatedly send up a quick prayer of thankfulness—my first one in a long time. *Thank you, God, for watching over me and helping me through this difficult time.*

~*~

Dropping off and picking up Sofie has become the highlight of my day. *Does a sweet teacher play a role in that?*

I dawdle in the back of the room, waiting for the other parents to clear out. After several minutes, it's finally just Sofie, me, and Rae.

"How did your day go?" I ask, even though I can see the tiredness in Rae's eyes and her usually tidy bun is drooping at the back of her neck.

A grin lights her pretty face. "I had too much fun over the weekend, so I'm having trouble getting back into the groove."

I laugh.

"Could you go out to dinner with Sofie and me? I have some good news to share with you."

An uncomfortable expression crosses Rae's face as she shifts nervously back and forth. "Noah, I'm sorry if I led you on by going out to dinner with you on Saturday. Principal Marshfield has a strict policy of no fraternization between teachers and parents. I told her this morning about working with you on the stained-glass project. While she agreed I could continue working on the project, she firmly re-iterated the 'no dating' policy." Her eyes plead with me for understanding.

Wow. This principal is strict to a fault. "I don't want to jeopardize your job, Rae. But can't we go out just as friends? Sofie will be there, so what would be the harm?"

She nervously clears her throat and speaks in such a low voice that I tilt my head towards her to hear her. "Noah, you're too much of a temptation." Rae bites her bottom lip and blinks furiously.

I grimace. *Well, isn't this a kick in the pants?* While I'm pleased at her admission to being attracted to me, my previous euphoria is tempered by this new news about the "no dating" rule. Still, that isn't the end of the world. "Sofie isn't going to be your student forever. I'm a patient man. I'll wait," I blurt out, then grin at my own knee-jerk admission.

A pink blush crawls up her neck and across her cheeks. A small smile tips up her lips at my declaration. "After speaking with Principal Marshfield, I called Pastor Tim and asked him if he could recruit another volunteer for the stained-glass work. I didn't tell him why, but I think it would be best if we had a buffer."

My grimace instantly reappears. *Or a third wheel.* I cut off my disparaging thoughts. "Oh, does he know of another volunteer?"

Rae nods. "June Clemson is going to join the team."

I scowl. "She tried to take over the stained-glass project last time. Her know-it-all attitude was a little much for me." Rae's eyes widen at my unfavorable review of our new project member.

Smoothing my face into a neutral expression, I reply, "Maybe she's changed. I'll give her a second chance. See you on Saturday." With that, I turn and leave, biting my tongue to cut off any further grumpy remarks.

"What's your good news?" Rae asks before I can get out the door.

I pause, wishing I could talk to her privately rather than in this classroom, but that probably breaks the rules, too. "Oh, it's nothing," I say in a brusque voice.

50

She frowns, disappointment at my abrupt reply showing in her pretty eyes.

I feel terrible that I unintentionally hurt her feelings. "Is there any rule that we can't talk on the phone or FaceTime?" The suggestion spills out my mouth.

Rae's face noticeably brightens. "I guess not."

I give her an encouraging smile. "Okay, then. I'll call you tonight and tell you my good news." After I get to my vehicle, I help Sofie into her safety seat and give myself a pep talk. There's only six more months of school, and then I can pursue the lovely Miss Dailey as much as I want. It strikes me that her name fits her perfectly. *Rae.* A ray of sunshine in my otherwise dull life.

"Daddy, can we get a kiddie meal?" Sofie asks once I've pulled out of the school parking lot.

"That's a great idea! Let's go get Aunt Ellie so she can join us."

Sofie claps and starts singing one of the *Frozen* songs.

Despite the "no dating" rule, today's been a fantastic day and it deserves a celebration. The call with Rae tonight is the next best thing to dating her. *I'll eventually convince myself that's true.* Humming along to the song, I sound like a devoted father who's seen the movie far too many times. *Yep. That's me.*

Chapter Eight

Raelynn

IT'S SUCH TERRIBLE LUCK TO have the first guy I'm attracted to in a long time be the father of one of my students. *Big-time bummer.*

I feel better after talking to Principal Marshfield, getting everything out in the open. No misunderstanding that might cause me to lose my job. But speaking with Noah about the school's "no dating" rule was more difficult than I thought. While he was understanding, I saw the disappointment on his face. The one bright spot is his call this evening, and I can't wait.

Eating dinner and puttering around the house, I kill time until the phone dings with a FaceTime request around eight o'clock. My heart does a summersault in my chest worthy of an Olympic gymnast.

"Hello," I say in a breathless voice, taking a few calming breaths.

"Well, hello to you, too. Sounds like you've been running," he says with a chuckle.

I blush like a schoolgirl. "Oh, I had to run upstairs to get my phone." *Just a little fib.*

He laughs. "I just tucked Sofie in. She started singing *Frozen* songs on the way home, so guess what movie we had to watch this evening?"

I laugh. "Um, let me guess . . . *Frozen*?"

He grunts. "Yeah. For the hundred and third time."

"You probably also know every song, then."

"Don't tell anyone. I may lose my man card."

I snicker. "Well, I'm on pins and needles. What's the good news?"

"Are you sitting down?"

My brows draw together. "Is it that good or is it that shocking that I need to sit?"

"A little of both."

I flop down on the sofa. "Okay, I'm sitting now. Let me have it."

He barks out a laugh. "First off, I got an offer on the house and accepted it."

Sitting up straighter, I say, "Noah, that's great news! It must be such a relief."

"Yes and no. I'm glad to get rid of that financial burden, but now I've got to find somewhere for Sofie and I to live. Ellie's going to move in over Twice Again where she works."

Wasn't one of the parents just talking about renting out a little cottage they own? I rack my brain to think of who said that. A light bulb goes on. "Mr. Peterson just mentioned to the other kindergarten teacher that he wants to rent a little cottage he owns. His renter just moved out. I'll tell Cassie to have him call you."

"Please do! I can't believe you remembered that."

I chuckle. "Mom always says I have a mind like a steel trap. You said this was the first piece of good news. What else happened?"

He clears his throat. "Uh, well . . . I sort of took your advice . . . I'm opening my own business to assist small businesses with all their finances. Ellie mentioned that Margaret who runs Twice Again is over her head with the financial side of the business. I met with her and she immediately signed on to my new venture. Plus, she gave me leads for more people to talk to." Noah's voice rises with excitement the more he talks. My heart warms for him. "Just a few months ago I wouldn't have considered starting a new business on my own."

"What did I tell you?"

"Um, what?" he sounds puzzled.

"God will guide you and everything will work out."

"Yeah, I've been trying to take your advice and listen to Him more. I guess it's working."

We talk for a few more minutes about all the exciting things that happened at school during my day. An urgent bathroom run, spilled paint, an altercation over a ball on the playground. *All the usual stuff.*

When I look at the clock, I realize we've been talking for almost an hour. "I better sign off and get to bed. Us kindergarten teachers have to get up at the crack of dawn."

Noah chuckles. "Sweet dreams."

I snuggle under the covers with a goofy smile on my face. I'll be dreaming about him for sure.

~*~

Saturday dawns, and it's raining cats and dogs (a cliché I recently taught my kindergarteners, and I can still hear their giggles). I look out the window and sigh, wishing I could spend all day inside, puttering around the house, baking cookies, and reading a book. The appointment with Frank, Noah, and June is in an hour, so I better get ready. I need to find my stained-glass supplies because they're still packed in a box in the basement—I haven't used them since I moved.

I'm already dreading working with June Clemson on the stained-glass windows if Noah's reaction was correct about her. But I trust God to guide me to joyfully accept June onto the team. There's no doubt I'm going to need His help on this one.

Pulling into the FaithBridge parking lot, I see three cars already parked near the door. I grab my umbrella, supplies, and laptop bag, sprinting to the door. *Woosh!* A burst of wind and rain accompanies me inside. Three pairs of eyes greet me as I make my hasty entrance.

Shaking the water from the umbrella, I approach the small group. Frank looks the same as he did the last time we saw him—in his overalls, with a beat-up ball cap on his head. A battered toolbox sits at his feet, and the big ladder is set up beside the stained-glass window. The way he keeps taking sneaky glances over at June makes me wonder if he's interested in her. *Frank and June?* My inner matchmaker flares to life.

Noah's hair still has droplets of rain on it, and his shirt is wet, causing it to cling to all his very fine muscles. *Rae, keep your mind on the project and not the handsome single dad.*

June is dressed as if she's going to church, in a flowery dress and high-heeled shoes. Her white hair is in a style reminiscent of how my mom used to fix her hair, complete with copious amounts of hairspray to hold it firmly in place.

I look down at myself. With me in my old khakis and a worn-out Henley shirt, we make quite the motley crew.

"Welcome, Rae! June was just telling us about her extensive knowledge of stained glass," Noah says with a slight twitch in his lips.

Relieved that I missed that, I smile and say, "Her experience will come in handy, I'm sure."

Noah stifles a laugh under a cough.

"It's too wet to take down a section today, but I'll inspect each one," Frank says, cutting off any more chitchat.

Noah assists Frank to position the ladder, and they converse about each section and how difficult or easy it will be to remove it. Some of the wood frame between sections has weathered badly, giving cause for concern.

June sits beside me as I attempt to type notes of the men's conversation into my laptop. Her snippets of conversation are distracting.

"You're the lady who sits in the last pew. I've seen you a couple of times at the Sunday service."

I feel remiss at my lack of introduction earlier, so I extend my hand. "Raelynn Dailey. Everyone calls me Rae."

She shakes my hand while looking me over from head to toe, making me feel like a gnat under a microscope. "That's such a lovely name, dear. I don't think I've ever known anyone named Raelynn before."

Smiling at her compliment, I say, "My grandfather's name is Ray and Mom's best friend is named Lynn. So, Mom combined the two."

June puts her hand on her heart. "How wonderful! My mother wasn't quite as original—I'm named after the month I was born in."

We both laugh.

"Would you like to join the FaithBridge Women's Auxiliary? We meet once a month and help out serving for funerals and weddings."

My eyes widen at the unexpected invitation. "Um, well, I teach kindergarten full time, so it might be difficult for me to help." June looks disappointed with my reply and I feel a twinge of guilt. "Could I be on a back-up list in case you get in a pinch?"

Her face immediately brightens. "I'll add you as a sub." She doesn't write anything down, so I wonder whether she'll remember. June tilts her chin towards the men. "That Noah sure is a nice-looking young man," she says.

I give her a sideways glance, wondering if she's trying to play matchmaker too, but her expression looks innocent enough. I reply with a non-committal grunt.

"It sure was nice of you to volunteer for this project," June continues.

I smile at this much safer topic. "I wanted to help and meet some new people at the same time."

June beams. "Well, it's nice to meet you as well, dear." That wasn't exactly what I meant, but I'm warming up to June despite her nosiness.

After several minutes, Noah and Frank join us, sitting in the pew behind where June and I are seated. "Frank has offered to take down the first section on the next dry day. I'll give him Pastor Tim's phone number so someone can meet him here if the rest of us are busy," Noah says.

I jot that down in the notes I've been taking.

"Someone needs to provide a tarp so I can button up the hole after I take out that section," Frank adds.

I nod and add a reminder in the notes to locate a tarp.

Now that the mundane stuff is done, June rises and claps her hands. "Who would like to join me at Sacred Grounds? They just added a line of sandwiches that I'm dying to try."

Frank clears his throat. "I'd love to join you."

Noah and I exchange a look, and I think we're both thinking the same thing. *Is there a romance brewing between these two?*

"I'll have to pass, I have an errand I need to run," I quickly reply. *Just stretching the truth a little since my errand is going home to do laundry.* I give Noah a pointed look that says he shouldn't crash Frank and June's date. Since Frank and June are in an animated conversation about cheddar versus Swiss cheese, I add a couple eye rolls and an elbow in the ribs until he finally catches on.

"Um, I have to pick Sofie up from a playdate," he says rather unconvincingly.

Frank collects his toolbox and escorts June out of the sanctuary. She flips open a blue flowered umbrella and they walk out underneath it.

"Well, that was a surprise," Noah comments as we prepare to leave.

"What was?"

He laughs. "Frank blushing like a teenager and June giggling at his lame jokes. He distracted June so much she didn't try to take over the project."

"I think it's sweet. They make a perfect pair. But didn't they both work last year on the entry windows?"

"Funny thing, I don't think they were ever at the church at the same time for that project."

I giggle. "Too bad, their romance could have started sooner."

The sides of Noah's eyes crinkle with laugh lines. "True! You know, we could have gone to lunch with them. Going out as a group doesn't break Principal Marshfield's rules, does it?"

I kick myself for not thinking of that sooner. "Maybe not. But let's give them time to get to know each other better first."

Noah senses my reluctance to any off-hours socializing with him, even with a group. "I respect your wishes, Rae. But just know that once the school bell rings on May 23, I'll be calling you for a date. That's only six months away."

He's looked up the date for the last day of school? I'm impressed. "I'll be waiting," I say with a grin.

We walk outside, and I share my umbrella with Noah, keeping him dry on the way to his car. He waves once I'm safely in my vehicle and follows me out of the lot.

My unexpected crush on Noah Sullivan grows bigger every time I see him. *What am I going to do to keep him at arm's length?*

Chapter Nine
Noah

THANKSGIVING SNUCK UP ON ME. My six new clients are keeping me busy, and I just today realized that Turkey Day is only three days away. I have so much to be thankful for this year. If you'd asked me a month ago, I would have been hard pressed to point to anything to be thankful for, but my life has changed. *Do I even miss my old life anymore?*

The house is almost packed, and we're moving on the Saturday after Thanksgiving. Pastor Tim insists that he can round up enough "strong bodies" to help move our stuff, so I rented a small moving van and trust that people will show up to help.

Ellie's already moved to the apartment over the store. Sofie and I miss her, but we're slowly adjusting to not having her around. I didn't know how much I depended on my sister for all kinds of things like: how much soap to put in the washer and where to put it, how to make a grilled cheese sandwich without charring it, how to braid hair so it stays in the braid for more than five minutes. I sigh. My dad skills are being tested, but I'm learning.

I've planned a little get together for the last Thanksgiving in my house. Ellie, along with her boss and my new client, Margaret, are both coming over for the big dinner. Since I've never fixed a turkey before, let's hope it doesn't turn out like the one in *Christmas Vacation.*

"Sofie! Time to go to the store. Get your shoes on." In my head, I hear Ellie teasing me that I left this chore to the last minute. *Hope they still have a good selection of turkeys.*

When we get to the grocery store, Sofie bounces beside me as we make our way through the aisles. The giant cart is over half full only a few aisles in. I swear they make the carts oversized, hoping you buy more stuff just to fill it up. Since I've never fixed Thanksgiving dinner before, I created a list on the grocery app on my cell and it's clutched in my hand so I can reference it often.

"Which one should we pick, Daddy?" Sofie says while we're standing beside the grocery cooler filled with frozen birds. I lean over and search through the case, picking the frozen birds up one at a time, reading the weight on the tag. Fifteen pounds. Twenty pounds. Twenty-three pounds. *How big of a bird do I need?*

"Trouble deciding, dear?"

Turning around, I see a diminutive white-haired lady standing beside me. Her cart is almost as full as mine.

I chuckle. "Is it that obvious?"

"Daddy's baking a turkey!" Sofie shouts as she dances around the lady and me. Heads turn as nearby shoppers laugh at my daughter's exuberance.

She bobs her white head. "You look a little like a deer caught in the headlights. How can I help?" My five-foot-one rescuer gives me a sweet smile while I corral Sofie, so she doesn't knock over the King's Hawaiian bread display.

"I'm not sure how many pounds to get," I say with a sheepish grin.

She laughs. "How many guests are you feeding? And do they all like turkey?"

My brows draw together. "Ellie likes turkey, but maybe Margaret prefers ham? Should I also get a ham?" I vocalize my thoughts.

"Margaret Thompson? Are you that nice Noah fellow she raves about?"

Surprise lights up my face at the compliment. "Yes, I'm Noah Sullivan." I extend my shake and we shake. "How do you know Margaret?"

"I own the quilt shop two stores down from Twice Again. I'm Grace McCallister. Do you think you could help me with my business finances? I hear you're a real whiz."

I pull out my wallet and hand her my business card. "I'd be happy to meet with you after Thanksgiving. Just give me a call."

Grace beams at the card like I handed her something precious. She carefully puts it in her purse. "Now, back to those turkeys. If you don't want a lot of leftovers, an eight- or ten-pound bird should suffice."

We dig through the case together, looking for a smaller bird. I finally find an eleven-pounder hidden near the bottom and quickly put it in my cart so no one else snatches it up.

"Thank you for your help, Grace. Don't forget to call me," I say as Sofie and I proceed with our shopping.

She waves. "I'll call next week."

"Is she a grandma?" Sofie asks once we're out of earshot. "I like her. Can she be my grandma?"

A stab of sadness hits me. *Wish Mom were still here so she could watch her beautiful granddaughter grow up.* "She's got her own family, but you still have Aunt Ellie."

Sofie's face lights up. "And Miss Dailey."

I smile and nod. *May 23 can't come fast enough.*

"Let's go figure out the difference between yams and sweet potatoes," I say as we approach the produce section. My extensive research said either would be appropriate for our meal.

~*~

My alarm goes off bright and early on Thanksgiving morning. I'm leaving myself plenty of time to get the turkey in the oven since I'm a rookie at this.

I get out the tin foil roaster pan that Grace instructed me to purchase—I'm so glad she did because I don't have any pans large enough to accommodate the eleven-pound bird.

Sofie joins me as I start preparing the turkey to put in the pan. My Google research said to look for the neck and a bag of giblets in the bird's cavities. I naively thought you just removed the wrapper and put the bird in the oven.

I wrestle to pull out the neck because the inside of the bird is still frozen. Sofie watches closely with inquisitive eyes. She scrunches up her little nose when I pull the horrid-looking thing out. Her eyes are big as saucers and she looks like she's going to cry. "What's that? Icky!" she squeals.

I almost blurt out "it's the neck" before I remember I'm speaking to a five-year-old. No need to have her cry for three hours over the reality of the turkey's demise. I quickly shove the ugly thing back into the cavity. "Just some spices to make the turkey taste yummy," I say.

Sofie looks skeptical, like she's going to ask more questions, so I quickly come up with a diversion. "Would you like to watch cartoons in the living room?" I usually don't allow my child to mindlessly watch TV, but this situation calls for a distraction and Ellie isn't here to help me.

"Yes!" Sofie jumps up and down at the unexpected offer, quickly forgetting the icky sight. "Peppa Pig, Peppa Pig," she sings as I find the show and leave her to watch it.

"We'll have some honey nut O's in a little bit," I say. She nods, already absorbed in the show.

Back in the kitchen, I work quickly to remove the neck and giblets, putting them in a white plastic bag and into the garbage. The bird's skin is much slipperier than I expected, so I hold on tight as I carefully place it in the pan. I can just imagine me dropping the turkey on the kitchen floor like that rerun episode from the TV show *Raymond* I saw just last week.

Inserting the meat thermometer (another utensil I had to purchase to prepare this meal) into the meaty breast, I pop the pan in the oven with a few minutes to spare on my carefully timed food preparation schedule. Mentally patting myself on my back, I call Sofie in to eat our cereal together.

~*~

Ellie arrives just in time to help with last-minute food prep. This meal is starting to stress me out because of everything you need to do at the same time. Make the gravy . . . Heat the rolls . . . Mash the potatoes. *How did Mom make this look easy?*

"What can I do to help?"

I glance at my list. "The turkey will need to rest for about five minutes once I pull it out. Can you mash the potatoes and I'll make the gravy when it's time?"

She nods.

We both peer through the oven glass window at the roasting bird. "The red thingy hasn't popped yet," I observe. Ellie smirks at my word choice. "What?" I say as she giggles. "Well, what do you call it?" I grumble. She continues to laugh at my expense but offers no other terminology I can add to my extensive turkey prep notes.

A sizzling noise draws our attention to the stovetop where the potatoes are boiling over for the second time. I run over, quickly turning the burner down, and cringe at the stove clean-up I'm going to have to do afterwards.

"It smells yummy, Noah. Did you stuff the bird?" My sister squints closer at the turkey in the oven because her favorite thing at Thanksgiving is the stuffing.

I point to the box sitting on the counter. "Is that okay?"

She laughs. "Sure. Maybe next year we can try Mom's stuffing recipe," she says wistfully. Mom did make the best stuffing.

The doorbell rings and Ellie rushes off to answer it. A few minutes later, Margaret wanders in carrying two pies. My daughter is chattering to her about the turkey. Hopefully she isn't describing the "icky thing" I pulled out earlier.

Over cereal, Sofie questioned me again about what that was. My unconvincing response about spices didn't sit well with her. The second time she asked, I told her it was something for making gravy and she seemed to accept that. *Oh, the joys of a five-year-old's curiosity.*

"Where should I put these, Noah?" Margaret asks. In the short time I've handled her business finances, she's become like a second mom to me. Margaret is quite the treasure.

I nod towards the island as I drain the water off the potatoes in the sink. The red thingy finally popped, and the thermometer read over the suggested temperature, so the bird's cooling on the counter, ready to carve. "Wherever you can find space."

She chuckles. "I'll mash the potatoes. And we need to get that gravy started," she says in an experienced-sounding voice. I'm grateful for the help.

It's all-hands-on-deck as we finish making the meal. I enjoy working beside Ellie and Margaret, who talk and laugh, helping me feel more confident that the meal is going to turn out okay. Sofie carefully folds the festive paper napkins I gave her to keep her busy.

When we sit at the table, I recheck my list to make sure we didn't forget anything.

"Butter for the rolls!" I exclaim as I run back to the kitchen for it. Mom always put the butter in a fancy dish, but I just plop the plastic margarine container on the table. *Oh well.*

"Let's say grace," I say once we're settled at the table. We join hands and I pray the simple prayer I researched on the internet—I didn't want to botch the prayer by trying to wing it.

"Amen," Ellie and Margaret both echo after me.

I look around the table and feel truly blessed. "Dig in!" I say as I pass the mashed potatoes.

~*~

My day isn't complete without my nightly FaceTime with Rae. We've been doing this for a couple of weeks now, and I'm hooked. Hearing her sweet voice and seeing her pretty face every evening is one of the highlights of my day. This will have to replace dating, for now.

"How did Thanksgiving with your parents go?" I ask after connecting the call. Rae's spending the holiday weekend at her childhood home in Denver.

She laughs. "Typical family meal. Mom made far too much food and my stepfather fell asleep in front of the TV afterwards."

I chuckle.

"I want to hear how your meal went," Rae says with excitement in her voice. I've been talking about the meal for days, so she knows how stressed out I was about it. "Did your extensive research pay off?" she teases.

I groan. She knows me too well, plus I may have mentioned my research a couple times too many. "Everything came out perfect. Although I almost traumatized my daughter when I pulled the neck out of the bird, but I made a quick recovery."

A loud belly laugh floats across the line. "Was it icky?"

Now it's my turn to laugh. "How did you know?"

"Ninety percent of things are icky to a five-year-old. My kids say it all the time. Seriously though, didn't you have any miscues? I would have if it were my first time fixing the big meal."

"Okay, honest confession time." I snicker at the memories of my "miscues," as Rae called them. "The yams were hard as rocks, so I had to microwave them, but they eventually got done. I forgot the fried onions in the green bean casserole, so we added them later with each person sprinkling them on top. And I forgot to buy whipped cream for the pumpkin pie. I swear it was on my list . . ." I mentally shrug, wondering how I missed that important item. "Margaret had some of that whipped cream in a can, so she rushed home and got it. Then Sofie sprayed it all over the table."

By this point, Rae's howling with laughter. I hear her snort a few times as well.

"It wasn't *that* bad," I say in a grumpy voice after she composes herself again.

"It's just the way you told it, Noah. Have you considered writing comedy?" Her soothing words have me smiling again in no time.

We talk about her shopping trip planned with her mom to hit up the Black Friday sales tomorrow. "You're still planning on the big move on Saturday, right?" she asks.

"Yep. I have my fingers crossed that people show up to help load and unload. Otherwise, it's up to me, Pastor Tim, and Sofie," I say with a nervous chuckle.

"Oh, with Pastor Tim involved, the volunteers will show. I can't wait to hear all about it."

Chapter Ten

Noah

MOVING DAY. LIKE I TOLD RAE, I won't be able to relax until the moving crew arrives and I know we have enough help to get all this stuff in the moving van I rented for the day. Considering I've lived in Paradise Springs for almost eight years, until recently my circle of friends could be counted on only a few fingers. Although I'm trying to mend my ways, I still don't have confidence that people will *volunteer* to give up their Saturday to help *me*.

I stare at the boxes littering every room in the house. Even after a garage sale and selling several things on Craigslist, our pile of stuff is still overwhelming. I bet it doesn't fit into the small bungalow I rented from the Petersons. Another round of downsizing is soon to come.

The doorbell rings at ten, and Pastor Tim smiles at me through the front door's beveled glass. When I open the door, I peer around him, looking for the moving crew. One skinny teenager and a hunched over elderly man hover behind him. My heart sinks, but I manage to hide the frown that wants to take over my face.

"Are you ready for us?" Pastor Tim asks in his jovial voice.

Nothing seems to get Tim down, so I mentally try to figure out how this ragtag crew is going to get the job done. Right as I'm starting to panic, two pickup trucks squeal into the driveway. Teenagers of all shapes and sizes tumble from the back, along with a couple burly looking men.

Pastor Tim slaps my back as he leans over and says in a low voice, "I bet we have everything moved and unloaded in an hour."

Speechless, I nod a couple times then come out of my shocked daze. "Come in and I'll show you what we have. Do you want to load the furniture first?"

The older gentleman is Buddy Green, and according to Tim he's an expert at tearing down and setting up electronics. I point him to the two TVs and an outdated, bulky desktop computer. He nods and starts fiddling with the wires.

The other two men introduce themselves but I instantly forget their names. They quickly start shouting out instructions to the energetic teens. Sofie huddles at my legs as we watch our possessions being efficiently brought out to the moving van. Pastor Tim declares himself an expert packer, and he directs where to put stuff in the van. The structured chaos around us is comforting in an odd way.

Less than an hour later I gaze across the empty house. The only reminder that we lived here are some indentations in the carpet where the heavy furniture previously sat. Sofie shrieks as we walk through the house, her voice echoing in the empty rooms.

"My voice sounds big," she says with a giggle.

I grasp her tiny hand as we make our way from room to room, making sure nothing was left behind. This house is too big for our needs. *What was I thinking when I bought it?* The granite countertops and high-end stainless-steel appliances in the kitchen mock me as we walk by. I purchased the six-burner Wolf range the first year in the house and used it about five times, including the recent Thanksgiving feast. My emphasis on having the best *things* eventually caught up with me. *What a wake-up call.* I do regret leaving Sofie's room behind. She loved the bright pink walls that Ellie helped me paint. Maybe Mr. Peterson will let me paint Sofie's room in the bungalow.

Once we've walked through the entire house, I pull a key off my keyring to hide under the front mat for the cleaning company. They're coming over tomorrow to make sure everything is spick and span for the new owner. They're familiar with the house because they've been cleaning the huge place weekly since I purchased it—except for recently, because I couldn't afford them anymore.

We join Pastor Tim at the front door. "Did we get everything?" he asks.

"Yeah, looks good."

"Do you want to follow in your vehicle? I'll drive the moving van," he says. His grin tells me that he can't wait to drive the oversized van with the stick shift.

I hand over the keys to the van to the happy pastor. "Follow me. The new place is just off Fifth street."

The pastor struggles using the clutch—the moving van lurches and leaps forward a couple times, the tires screeching against the pavement, until the engine dies. From my car's rearview window, I watch tech guru Buddy try to suppress a grin from the passenger seat. After two attempts, Pastor Tim gets the hang of the manual transmission and the van moves smoothly. Suppressing my own laughter, I wait for the truck to pull up behind me and we head out.

~*~

Many hands make light work. Thank you, Lord, for all these kind people. That prayer of gratitude pops into my head as I stare across the sea of boxes and furniture stuffed into my tiny new home. I'm still surprised everything fit. The crew had everything moved and unloaded in just under two hours. *And I thought it would take all day.*

I order pizza and bring out the six packs of sodas and bottled water that I purchased. Although there isn't much seating, everyone finds a place to perch to eat—either on the floor or the furniture scattered around the room. Sofie sits on my lap and watches everything with wide eyes. She hasn't seen this many people in our house before.

Ten large pizzas are consumed in a few minutes by the hungry crew. The boisterous teens laugh and talk in between bites. Ellie stops by with a pan of brownies, and in seconds there's only crumbs remaining.

"Noah, what do you do?" the man named John asks, as he nibbles on a brownie.

"I help small businesses run the financial side of their business. Do their accounting, taxes, payroll, stuff like that." Funny how quickly my confidence in my new business has grown and I can talk about it as if I've been doing this for years. Robertson Industries and the allure of working for a large corporation is firmly behind me. It just occurs to me that I don't even miss my old life anymore.

The other man, Darryl, pipes up, "My brother is a mechanic and runs a small auto repair place. He could really use your help."

Pulling my wallet out of my pocket, I hand him a business card. "Have him set up an appointment. I'd be happy to see if I can help." Surprisingly, I haven't had to spend a dime for marketing or advertising yet. *Word of mouth is proving to be powerful—and best of all, it's free.*

Pastor Tim starts collecting trash, and everyone pitches in to help with clean up. In a matter of minutes, the room is clean and the moving crew departs as quickly as they arrived.

Once everyone clears out, Ellie exhales a loud breath. "Noah, you've still got too much stuff. Where are we going to put everything?"

I laugh. "Hold another garage sale? Donate some more stuff?"

She puts her hands on her hips. "I have first dibs on Mom's old mixer."

"It's yours, sister. You've just got to find it."

We both laugh.

"You don't need to stick around," I add.

She squeezes my arm. "Let's worry about getting the two bedrooms set up first. Then I'll leave you to it," Ellie says as we head to the bedrooms.

Hours later, after talking to Rae and updating her on the move, I lay in bed, staring at my new ceiling. I haven't lived in a house with a popcorn ceiling for a long time. *Would the owner let me remove it for him?*

My heart swells with emotion that all those kind-hearted people helped me today. They don't even know me. Plus, I'm not even technically a member of Pastor Tim's church. Guess he feels some obligation to help me based on my assistance with the stained-glass window.

For the first time in a long time, I remember to say my evening prayers, just like Mom taught me. *God, thank you for sending help my way today. Amen.*

Chapter Eleven

Raelynn

EVEN THOUGH THE WEATHER HAS turned cooler, Frank wants to try to remove and repair one of the stained-glass sections today. It's a bright and sunny Saturday—Colorado has the most stunning blue skies when the sun shines. With the backdrop of the snow-covered mountains, you'd swear you were living in an idyllic oil painting. I itch to get out my paint brush and try to capture the scene, but there isn't time before I meet everyone at the church.

When I arrive, Noah pulls in right beside me. We grin at each other as we get out of our vehicles. The other two cars in the lot must be Frank and June. I pop my trunk and get out my supplies.

"Let me help you carry those," Noah says as he takes the box from me. When our fingers touch, a tingle runs up my arm. "By the way, I like the new look," he says as he nods towards my new haircut.

A blush heats my face. "I got tired of hair falling out of a bun or ponytail, so this is much easier." The shoulder length cut is perfect; I don't know why I didn't do it sooner.

We enter the sanctuary where Frank and June are sitting in the front pew. Both are oblivious to our presence because they're in an animated discussion. As we get closer, my eyes widen. Frank's usual attire has been replaced with a pressed button-down shirt and khaki pants. His hair has been combed, and he even shaved his face. June is in her same flowery dress, but her sturdy, chunky heels have been upgraded to a pair of flattering, although terribly impractical, stiletto-style heels.

Noah elbows me and whispers, "Looks like those two are flirting."

Right as he says those words, Frank sees us and waves. "'Bout time you two got here," he says in his gruff voice.

June hops to her feet and gives first Noah and then me a hug. "My, you two sure do make a cute couple," she says with a wink.

"We aren't a couple," Noah and I both say, the words rushing out our mouths at the same time. Our denial sounds a little too vehement to be believable.

Frank snorts.

June walks over and turns my head from side to side. "Rae, dear, your new haircut is so becoming on you," she says after her inspection.

"Thank you, June," I reply while the two men look bored with the hair discussion. Clearing my throat and changing the topic, I say, "I'm ready to work on the window." I point towards the box still grasped in Noah's hand.

That comment spurs Frank into action. "I thought I'd remove only the first section right now and see how that goes. Once I have it out, we can start working on it over there." He motions towards two sawhorses and a large piece of plywood set up in the corner, creating a makeshift worktable. Noah sets my box near the table.

Frank climbs the tall ladder and uses a wedge-looking device to pry the first section's frame out while making sure not to disturb the next section. It's a slow process, so Noah takes over after about half an hour. The men trade positions back and forth as they slowly work their way down the frame, prying it out. June fills the time with conversation mostly bordering on gossip, although I don't remember much of what she said.

The hope is that the wooden frame is still sturdy, so that the glass doesn't fall out while we work on it and that it won't sustain any additional damage during the removal. I didn't realize the process would be so delicate and slow. I hold my breath when the frame pops out away from the rest of the window. Noah grabs the top from his position on the ladder and Frank catches the bottom. Then they slowly carry the window over to the worktable.

Next Frank and Noah hang the tarp that I purchased several weeks ago to cover the opening. They tack it up with small nails, the bright blue tarp looking out of place beside the rest of the beautiful window. Part of the sanctuary is now dark without the sunlight streaming in.

"This should hold until we get the first section repaired," Noah says as he climbs off the ladder. Frank nods.

The four of us carefully examine the glass. I pull out the grid I created several weeks ago with Noah and rattle off the damage to this section that we previously identified. Noah, Frank, and June note any other areas needing repair.

"I can repair the lead strips," I say as we formulate a plan. The glass in stained-glass windows is joined together with strips of lead soldered at the joints, and the window is then grouted with putty to glaze and seal it. Over time, the putty dries and falls out and the lead then has room to stretch and weaken. I'll carefully remove the decayed parts of the lead strips, adding new lead in its place.

"Since there's so much lead damage, I'll help Rae," Noah says.

"June and I will tackle the cracks," Frank adds while June nods.

We grab our supplies and begin work. The section is large enough such that all four of us can work on it at the same time and not get in each other's way. Noah and I start at the top, with Frank and June at the bottom, working towards each other.

I lose track of time as I focus on the work. Noah and I make a good team, while Frank and June appear to do the same. We're quite an efficient crew, although the work is slow and tedious. We converse quietly in our two-person groups, discussing the repair we're making and giving each other advice. Fortunately, between all four of us, we have the experience and expertise needed for the job.

Bam!

The church's massive front door slams loudly and we all jump. Pastor Tim waves and strides up the aisle towards our work area. He has several white paper sacks in his hands, along with a tray of drinks.

"I brought food!" he says in his booming, cheerful voice.

A glance at the clock on the back wall shows 12:15, which means we've been working for over four hours. *Boy, I sure lost track of time.*

The aroma of hamburgers and French fries wafts from the white bags. My stomach growls as if on cue. Noah winks when he hears the embarrassing noise.

Pastor Tim spreads out the lunch on the coffee serving counter located in the breezeway between the sanctuary and the Sunday school rooms. The men haul out some folding chairs so we can sit and eat.

The rustling of food wrappers fills the room. "Shall we pray?" Pastor Tim says. Everyone stops unwrapping the food, a little embarrassed at our lack of manners. "Dear Lord, thank you for this food. May we use it to nourish our bodies. Bless these generous people who are repairing our church window, giving of their time and expertise. Through Jesus Christ our Lord and Savior. Amen."

Everyone joins in the Amen then proceeds to eat. The hamburgers are still warm and the sodas ice cold—a tantalizing combination.

"This really hits the spot," Frank says after snarfing down his hamburger. He picks up a second burger and adds ketchup from the little packets strewn across the table.

We all murmur our agreement.

After the tasty meal, we update Pastor Tim on our progress. He looks over the first section as we tell him what we're doing. "This is amazing. You're doing a wonderful job. How long will this section take?"

"We're over half done. Our goal is to try to get it done today and reinstalled, so no one damages it at tomorrow's services," Noah says.

The pastor nods. "Well, I better leave you to carry on then. Thank you for all your hard work," he says as he collects our garbage and leaves.

"He's sure a nice fellow," Frank comments as we resume our positions around the window.

"A real blessing to our church," June chimes in.

"His appreciation makes all our hard work worth it," I say.

"The guy makes you want to do anything for him. No wonder he's so successful at getting volunteers to help around the church," Noah adds.

Frank chuckles. "If he was a salesman, he could sell ice cubes to Eskimos."

Everyone laughs, then gets back to work.

Six hours later, I stretch my aching back while Frank and Noah reinstall the repaired window. It glistens and looks vibrant, just like new, beside the other sections. The pristine window inspires us to get the three remaining sections completed as soon as possible.

"How about we try to get this job done before the Christmas Eve service?" Noah suggests as we're standing around admiring our work.

"That would be wonderful! Pastor Tim would be so excited to unveil the completed window at the service," June says.

I swipe and bring up the calendar on my phone, noting that we've got only two more weekends to work on the project. "We may have to work on a few weeknights to get it done since this bit took ten hours," I remind everyone.

"We should be able to work faster now that we have some experience under our belts," Frank says and the group nods in agreement. "If we start earlier, we could do two sections on one of the Saturdays," Frank suggests.

"I might have to bring a five-year-old with me," Noah warns.

June claps her hands delightedly. "Oh, please do!" Everyone laughs except for curmudgeon Frank.

Heads nod and we agree to the schedule for the next two Saturdays. I'm especially looking forward to the plan. Working with Noah on this project is the next best thing to dating him. Plus, we have built-in chaperones with Frank and June. *Or maybe Noah and I are chaperoning them?*

As we all walk to our cars, I realize just how tired I am. I may have to attend the late church service tomorrow. 9:00 a.m. sounds early to me right now.

Noah loads my box of supplies back into my trunk. "We make a great team, Rae," he says with a flirty sparkle in his eyes as he walks away.

Whew! That man makes my heart do flips. I can't wait for May 23 either.

Chapter Twelve

Noah

CHRISTMAS HAS NEVER BEEN MY favorite time of year. In fact, the old Noah would grumble about all the fuss. Now I'm as invested as the jolly white-haired man himself.

Ellie helps me string lights all along the front porch. "When did you start decorating for Christmas?" Ellie teases.

I chuckle from my position on the ladder. "Have you seen this neighborhood? My house sticks out like a sore thumb with no lights. Peer pressure is a powerful thing."

My sister barks out a laugh. "And is peer pressure making you go buy a tree? That's all Sofie can talk about."

Busted. I made the mistake of telling my daughter where we're going this afternoon.

I shrug nonchalantly at Ellie's teasing and peek in the front window to make sure the loudmouthed little sprite hasn't gotten into any trouble, but she's still happily watching *Elf*.

Ellie and I double-check the lights once they're installed to make sure all are still working. I did a thorough check before putting them up because I didn't want to be like Chevy Chase in *Christmas Vacation*. The lights pass inspection and I smile at how festive the red and white twinkle lights are going to make my front porch look.

"Want to go to lunch with Sofie and me before we head over to the tree lot? I owe you for helping with the lights."

"Sure, I'd love to. How about we try that new sandwich shop that opened just down from Twice Again? I haven't had time to try it yet."

"Sounds good. Sofie and I'll meet you there in half an hour. It'll take me that long to get her ready."

Ellie nods and waves as she drives off.

"Sofie, we're going out to lunch with Aunt Ellie," I say as I walk back into the house.

She shakes her head and pouts. "But my movie isn't done yet." Her voice sounds whiny, and she gives me the "I'm not doing it" Sofie look.

Hoping to head off a confrontation with my sometimes-stubborn daughter, I pause the DVD for a second and determine that there's only fifteen minutes left in the film. "Okay, you can watch the rest and then we'll go."

Sofie grins as I resume the show. I decide to watch with her, and soon we're both laughing at Will Ferrell's antics. I'd forgotten how funny this movie is.

We stroll into Sandwiches and Stuff thirty-five minutes later. I mentally pat myself on the back that we're only a few minutes late. Ellie waves from a booth in the corner. A waitress comes over immediately as if she were trailing me on the way in. *Wow, they have fast service here.*

Quickly scanning the menu, I order for Sofie and me. When Ellie orders a sandwich made with organic sprouted rye bread, I don't ask about what that really means. After the overly anxious waitress leaves, my sister says, "What kind of tree are you going to get?"

"A Christmas tree!" Sofie exclaims.

Ellie laughs. "What I meant was, are you going to select like a Fraser fir, Douglas fir, or balsam fir."

I give my sister a clueless look. *Was I supposed to research types of Christmas trees?*

She reaches across the table and pats my hand. "No worries, Noah. Just go with your gut and get the one you and Sofie like the best."

I nod but remind myself to do a little Googling on my phone when we get to the tree lot. I can't go in unprepared.

"Do you have any decorations?"

"Yes, I didn't forget those. Sofie and I went shopping last week."

"I got a stocking, too!" Sofie says. Unfortunately, there were tears when she got home and realized we don't have a fireplace. So, I told Sofie that Santa uses a window if there's no chimney. The stocking is now proudly hanging beside the front bay window.

"Did you remember a tree stand?" Ellie asks with a smirk.

"What? Do you take me for a Christmas novice?" I say, then scribble a note in my phone to get one of those at the tree lot. After we're digging into the tasty sandwiches, I change the subject. "How's the new employee?"

A frown crosses Ellie's face. "Riley works hard, but she sticks to herself. She doesn't make any attempt to get to know me or Margaret better. I don't know what's up with her."

The words hit a little too close to home. Makes me wonder what the other employees at Robertson Industries thought of me. "Give her time, I'm sure she'll come around."

Ellie shrugs. "At least she's a whiz at refinishing furniture and very knowledgeable about antiques."

Sofie hands me her dill pickle. "I don't like that, Daddy."

I chuckle and put it on my plate. "Do you like your grilled cheese, sweet pea?" Sofie nods and takes a big bite out of her standard-fare sandwich. "Make sure you eat your apple slices too." She ignores my comment and sneaks a few potato chips from my plate.

"How's the new business? I heard that Grace McCallister is your new client," Ellie resumes the conversation between bites.

"Yep, her quilting shop is my seventh client already. And to think I met her when I was selecting our Thanksgiving turkey."

We both chuckle.

"That's terrific, Noah. Got any other leads on new clients?"

I bemusedly shake my head. "One of the guys who helped us move has a brother who owns an auto repair business. I'm meeting with him next week." I continue to be amazed at how my little start-up business is thriving due to word of mouth. It's truly a miracle, and I feel God's help in making this happen.

Lord, thank you for my many blessings, including my new clients. May I help them and their businesses.

When we're done eating, I pay for lunch, hug my sister, and head to the Christmas tree lot. I'll do a little research when we get there, and hopefully they'll have a tree stand I can purchase.

~*~

"Ever heard the saying 'You don't know what you don't know'?" I ask Rae during our nightly phone call.

She laughs and replies, "Oh yes, I'm all too familiar with that. My kindergarteners remind me of the fact every day."

I love how I feel totally comfortable confessing my shopping blunders to Rae. "Well, today was one of those days. I thought I had done all my research and was quite prepared for the tree shopping, but then Ellie threw a wrench in everything when she asked me what *type* of tree I was getting."

An unladylike snort floats across the line. Rae knows my tendency to over-research everything. "And what *type* did you get?"

I groan. "My research said that the noble fir was best for not shedding needles. But when we looked at one, neither Sofie nor I liked how it looked. They're tall and skinny, not full like a normal Christmas tree."

Giggles resonate over the line.

"We ended up ignoring all my research and just picked the one we liked best." *So much for research and preparation.*

"Well?"

"Well, what?"

"What type did you get?" Rae says, enunciating slowly so I finally catch on.

"Oh, yeah, that. The tag says it's a Douglas fir," I say with a loud sigh, since my research said those are the worst for shedding needles. Looking at the tag was an afterthought once I got the tree home.

"Oh, Noah. You're so cute."

Um, not sure I like the term *cute*—I hope she means handsome and funny. "My sister also reminded me that I needed a tree stand, which luckily they had at the tree lot. One thing led to another, and the teenage salesgirl there sold me an embroidered tree skirt, an angel tree topper, and two stuffed reindeer to sit beside the tree because Sofie just had to have them. When all was said and done, I was out over two-hundred bucks."

The giggling on the other end resumes, and in fact it gets louder. After a few beats Rae says, "Just a second, I need to grab a tissue to wipe my eyes from all this laughing."

Way to make a guy feel about two feet tall.

"I'm back." *Giggle. Giggle. Giggle.* "So, after all that, how'd the decorating go?"

"Oh, I couldn't handle anymore *learning* today, so we're going to decorate the tree tomorrow. I'll get back to you on how that goes."

More giggles and a loud blowing of the nose follow my words. *Guess I'm more entertaining than I thought.*

When we sign off, I have a smile on my face despite the frustrations I was feeling earlier. Rae makes every day brighter. I send up a much overdue prayer of gratitude thanking God for bringing her into my life.

Chapter Thirteen

Raelynn

IT'S THE LAST SATURDAY BEFORE Christmas Eve and we're doing the big push on repairing the stained-glass window. Today we're tackling the final two sections—it's going to be a long day.

Frank and June are already working on removing the last sections when I arrive. Noah isn't here yet, but that's no surprise because Sofie's coming with him. His daughter will be here until Ellie gets off work sometime this afternoon.

"Good morning! Anyone want coffee?" I hold up the tray containing four paper coffee cups.

"You're a lifesaver, Rae," June says as she abandons Frank while he's still up on the ladder. She comes over and grabs the cup marked *June*. Hers is a blend of cinnamon and cayenne pepper. You wouldn't think those two flavors would go together in a coffee, but they work.

Frank grumbles as he climbs down, giving June a pointed look. She shrugs and continues sipping the hot brew. *Is there trouble brewing in paradise with these two?* (pun intended) I hand him the plain black coffee marked with his name. None of those fancy flavors for him.

The front double doors fly open and Noah rushes in. Sofie's tagging behind him looking cranky and sleepy.

"Sorry I'm late. We had a little trouble getting up this morning." A subtle head movement indicates it was the pint-sized girl who's the reason for their tardiness.

June and I laugh quietly while I hand Noah his coffee cup. He smiles and immediately starts sipping.

Sofie hides behind Noah's legs, looking everyone over. He pulls her forward and makes introductions. "Sofie, this is June and Frank."

June waves. Frank shocks me when he walks over to Sofie and bends down to her height. "Pleased to meet you, young lady," he says and extends his hand. Sofie chews on her thumb for a second, looking him over from head to toe, then extends her tiny hand. They shake and both grin from ear to ear.

After the touching scene, I come over and hand Sofie a white paper bag. "Thought you might like this."

Her eyes light up and she hugs my legs. "I'm so glad to see you, Miss Dailey!" With that greeting, you'd think it had been a week since we last saw each other rather than one day.

Noah points to a pew and Sofie sits down, then opens her bag. She squeals with delight and pulls out a carton of chocolate milk and a blueberry muffin. Noah smiles at me and says, "That's perfect since we didn't have time for breakfast. What do you say to Miss Dailey, Sofie?"

With her mouth stuffed full of muffin Sofie replies and it sounds like "tunks."

Frank points to the ladder. "Shall we get started? There's a lot to do today."

Noah takes another quick sip, then joins Frank by the window and over the next half hour they proceed to remove the next two sections. Both are getting much faster at this process.

June and I sit next to Sofie and enjoy the rest of our coffee as we watch the men work. "How old are you, Sofie?" June asks once Sofie's finished her muffin. She holds up five fingers. June looks appropriately impressed. "My granddaughter is six; maybe you can meet her sometime." Sofie's eyes widen, and she nods her head excitedly.

This is all news to me. "Where does your granddaughter live?"

"Near Denver, but she visits all the time."

"That's nice, I'm sure," I say.

Obvious delight lights up June's face. "I have one granddaughter and three grandsons," she adds with pride.

After Sofie's done with her treat, she gets restless, so I find her bag and pull out her tablet. "Is there a game you want to play?"

"Yes!" she wiggles her fingers and I hand her the tablet. She's got the game up and playing in a matter of seconds.

June shakes her head in amazement. "She's a lot more proficient on that thing than I am."

I giggle to myself at how true that statement is. My kids surprise me all the time at their skills with technology.

When the guys bring the sections over to the two sets of worktables, June and I join them. As per the previous weekends, Noah and I team up, as do Frank and June. We talk quietly in our small pairs, just enough conversation to discuss the repairs. Noah glances over to Sofie and she's still absorbed in the game.

The repairs are tedious but we're making good progress. A small hand tugs on my pantleg and I look down to see Sofie. She tugged on both Noah and my legs, so we both respond at the same time. "What do you need, Sofie?"

"I want a puppy," she says loudly, as if that's the most important thing right now. Noah and I exchange an amused look. "Angela's getting a puppy for Christmas. It's a Doodle, and I want one too." There's a touch of grumpiness in Sofie's voice, so I get the feeling that Noah and she have already discussed this. She stares at me with a small pout on her face.

"Now's not a good time to talk about this, Sofie. We're busy," Noah explains.

She screws up her face, stomps her foot, and wails. The noise echoes around the sanctuary. June saves the day as she says,

"Sofie, can you help me get everyone's lunch order? You and I can go get food in a little bit."

Sofie stops mid-cry. June instructs her to ask each person what they want while June writes down the order. Forgetting about the puppy, Sofie goes around the table getting the orders. June winks at Noah and he mouths "thank you." When Sofie gets to Frank, he bends down and says, "What's on the menu?"

A puzzled expression crosses Sofie's face. "Hamburgers, Mr. Frank," she replies. The group chuckles.

"Okay, I want mustard, ketchup, and pickles on mine."

Sofie leans in and whispers to him, "I don't like pickles." She then takes another tack, hoping for a new ally. "Do you think I can get a puppy?"

Frank looks like he swallowed his tongue but recovers quickly. "That's something for your dad to decide." Sofie nods sadly at the realization that she doesn't have an ally in Frank either.

Noah hands June the keys to his SUV since Sofie's still required to sit in a car seat. "Do you need my help getting her into the seat?"

"No, I do it all the time with my granddaughter." June extends her hand to Sofie. "Okay, Miss Sofie. Let's go get lunch for this hungry crew." She helps Sofie get her coat on and they leave.

After they're gone, Frank turns to Noah. "One of my dogs just had puppies. They aren't a fancy breed, but the mom is real nice and the puppies are cute. If you want to bring Sofie out to the farm and pick one out, you can."

Noah's eyes widen. "That's a generous offer, Frank."

He shrugs. "Every kid needs a dog. Teaches them responsibility and gives them a built-in buddy."

"You're a wise man, Frank," I say.

"Let me make sure my rental allows pets and I might take you up on the offer," Noah adds.

Frank smiles and gets back to work. There's a softie hiding behind that gruff exterior.

~*~

It's 8:00 p.m. and we just completed the second window. I stretch, trying to get the kinks out of my back while Noah and Frank reinstall the sections. June just left because of a previous commitment. Sofie had the woman wound around her little finger by the time they returned with lunch. June bought her two kiddie meals so Sofie could get both toys. It was fortunate that Ellie picked up Sofie about four hours ago because Sofie had run out of games and was getting cranky.

All our heads turn when the front doors whoosh open and Pastor Tim strides in. "Saw the lights were still on, so I just had to come and check on things." He stops beside me as we watch the final section going back up.

"The windows look amazing," he says with pride and awe in his voice.

"I agree. It was worth all the effort. Now the members can enjoy them for years to come," I say.

He nods and quietly admires the gorgeous restored window. Noah and Frank put the ladder away and then stand beside us as we all marvel at the sight.

"I'm planning a special service for Christmas Eve and want you all to attend," the pastor says.

We nod affirmatively, because who could turn down Pastor Tim?

As we're leaving, I hear Noah arrange with Frank a time to look at the puppies. I grin, knowing that will make Sofie an incredibly happy girl.

"You're a good man, Noah," I say as he lugs my supply box to the car. I stop and turn to him. "When I first met you, I thought you were a terrible dad. Sofie had been in my class for almost two months and I'd never seen you drop her off or pick her up one time." He tries to say something, but I hold up my hand. "I know getting fired was difficult, but I'd say it was a blessing in disguise. God had a better plan for you."

Noah's eyes crinkle at the corner as he smiles. "He did, and I thank Him every day for putting me on the right path." He pauses and gazes into my eyes as if trying to read my inner thoughts. "I also thank Him for putting you in my path, Miss Dailey."

My heart does a little flip in my chest at not only Noah's words but also the intense look he gives me.

"May 23," I mutter under my breath as I get into my car and drive away.

Chapter Fourteen
Noah

DING! DONG!

As I'm getting ready to visit my potential new client, the doorbell rings. It's before 9:00 a.m. and I'm not expecting anyone. When I see who's standing at the door, my brows draw together, and my heart rate increases. *This can't be good news.*

Opening the door just wide enough for me to peer out, I say, "Mr. Robertson, I wasn't expecting you."

The CEO of Robertson Industries smiles and nods, then says in a friendly voice, "You're a tough one to keep up with, Noah! I went to your last known address and the lady there said you'd moved. Luckily, she knew your new address. May I come in?"

When you get fired from your job, you can't afford the big fancy house anymore. I bite my lip so I don't vocalize those thoughts.

"Sure, please come in." I step aside and motion for him to take a seat in the living room. His eyes widen at the messy room, but I won't apologize for it. As surreptitiously as possible I remove the fuzzy pink bunny slippers from the coffee table, setting them on the floor underneath. Sofie's stuffed elephant and a doll lay on one of the end tables. *My house looks lived in.*

Bob sits on the couch and I sit across from him on the loveseat. "How may I help you, Mr. Robertson?"

He chuckles. "Oh, please call me Bob! Looks like you're ready for Christmas," he says as he nods towards the overly decorated tree. Sofie and I didn't know when to stop. The branches droop from all the ornaments. The angel leans sideways. Even though I've straightened the topper several times, it refuses to stand upright like the ones in those Hallmark movies. He stares at the two stockings hanging beside the window but doesn't comment. A Daddy stocking has joined Sofie's stocking because she was worried Santa would forget me.

Clearing his throat, Bob says, "I won't beat around the bush, Noah. Our internal investigation into the embezzled money has concluded. David was siphoning off money and hiding it in other accounts only he had access to. He was fired last month, so I'm looking for another CFO, and your name popped to the top of the list."

My eyes widen and my mouth hangs open for a couple of seconds. This is the last thing I expected Bob to say. I'm rooted to the spot and speechless. An annoyed feeling also enters my thoughts. *The investigation was completed over a month ago, and no one from Robertson Industries had the courtesy to tell me I was found innocent?* When my brain sputters back into gear, I say, "But you fired me, Bob. Surely that doesn't look good on my record."

He waves his hand in a dismissive fashion. "Technically we laid you off, Noah. And I'm here because we want you back . . . You'll report directly to me this time."

He now wants to call it a layoff? He's taking a lot of leeway with semantics. Expelling a loud breath through my nose at his phony claim, I choose to ignore the inaccuracy of his words. "I've started my own business and it's doing well. I don't see myself returning to the corporate world." The firm commitment to my fledgling business surprises even me, because just a few months ago I would have jumped at Bob's offer.

Bob steeples his fingers under his chin, a serious expression on his face. "Let me sweeten the pot, Noah. We'll pay you for all the months you missed, and you'll get a raise on day one."

My mind spins with dollar signs and starts to calculate the three months' backpay. *That would be a substantial amount.* When I don't respond, Bob adds, "For good measure, I'll make it six months' backpay. That's a nice round number." He sinks back into the sofa cushions, folds his hands in his lap, and waits for my answer. The confident expression on his face indicates that he's certain money will lure me back.

I wasn't kidding when I said I don't see myself back in the corporate world. When we moved, I gave away most of my button-down shirts and suits to the church. Pastor Tim runs an organization that helps unemployed men prepare for interviews, including getting them the right clothes, so my suits went to a good cause. I rub the stubble on my face as I ponder this surprising and lucrative offer.

Bob nods towards my chin, "Your new look would have to go. We still have the no beards policy." He then laughs as if he told a joke.

I nod, knowing that the beard is not a deal breaker in this case—but my clients are. Mrs. McCallister's smiling face bursts into my head. She's so grateful for my help with her business finances that she's stopped by a couple of times with Christmas cookies. The elaborately decorated gingerbread cutouts were delicious and delighted Sofie and me. Truth is, all my clients need me, and my expertise frees them from grappling with the financial aspects of their business that none of them excel at. This new venture has already rewarded me in so many non-monetary ways.

When I was struggling to make ends meet, did Robertson Industries reach out to check on me or to help me? I know I didn't make any effort to make friends when I worked there, but do I want to work for a cutthroat company that fires you like a disposable piece of equipment then begs you to come back only when it's beneficial for them?

I'm doing exactly what I'm supposed to be doing. A warm, contented feeling of satisfaction flows through my body once I arrive at my decision. Leaning forward on the loveseat, I look Bob directly in the eyes. "I appreciate the offer, but I'm happy doing what I'm doing now. I won't be returning to Robertson Industries."

The look on Bob's face is priceless, as if I'm the first person to ever turn him down. "But are you making as much money with your little business as I'm offering you?"

His innuendo that my "little business" is trivial and pointless sets my teeth on edge. Granted I'm not making as much money as I did before, but my life is so much more fulfilling. *My decision is made.*

Before I can speak, Bob rushes on. "Why don't you think about it for a couple days Noah? Don't make a rash decision."

Feeling completely at peace, I say, "I'm not making a rash decision, Bob. I've worked long and hard these past months to build my business from the ground up, and my clients all need my help. It's extremely gratifying."

He shakes his head in disappointment and unfolds his tall frame from the couch. "Sorry you won't be coming back. If you ever change your mind, give me a call."

I stand and walk with him to the door. As he turns to leave, I say, "Bob, when you fired me, it was one of the lowest points of my life. In the three months since, you never reached out one time. All this time I lived in fear that David would pin the crime on me and you'd have me arrested."

He grimaces at my blunt words. "Firing you was not my finest moment. And we probably owed you an update that you were found to not be involved." He clears his throat. "But I hope we can move on from that. Even if you don't return to the company, I'd like to know that there's no bad feelings between us."

I shake his hand. "I've forgiven you, Bob. God showed me the kindness of so many people in my time of need. I hope He guides you to do the same for someone in need."

The tall white-haired gentlemen nods and walks to his car. I can only hope that my words made an impact.

~*~

Evans Auto Body and Repair is hopping when I arrive for my appointment with the owner. The receptionist points me to Logan Evans, who's busy conferring with someone about their car—a souped up Corvette with shiny red paint. My teenage-self eyes the car with longing. Standing off to the side, I wait for the conversation to end.

"You must be Noah? I'm Logan," the owner says. He's a strapping guy sporting a bushy beard who's at least a head taller than my six feet. He looks like a mountain man, and his booming voice reminds me of Pastor Tim. We shake hands, then he motions to the right. "Follow me to my office."

We wind our way around different vehicles in various stages of being serviced and end up in a small cubbyhole in the back corner of the garage. The cramped space barely qualifies as an office. Logan squeezes behind the desk while I take the straight-backed chair shoehorned in front of it. My eyes widen as I take in the disarray. Papers are stacked everywhere.

Logan chuckles at my shocked expression. "I never get around to organizing anything." His Captain Obvious comment amuses me. He stretches his arm to a bookcase beside the desk and pulls out a box stuffed full of more papers. "These are the important papers," Logan says with a grin.

"What are these other papers?" I ask waving towards the stacks on the desk.

He shrugs. "Service orders that have been completed. But I have receipts for every payment in the box," he says proudly, as if that's quite an accomplishment.

Letting out a small sigh, I say, "Do you have any of these papers entered into your bookkeeping software?"

"Yeah, all of them from last year. My cousin's wife did those last December. Haven't had anyone to enter these yet."

My eyes widen further. *So, the box represents almost twelve months of receipts and invoices?* "How are you paying invoices for expenses that are due?"

Logan shrugs. "I write a check when the bill comes in and note it in the checkbook log." He flips open the checkbox resting on top of the papers in the box and shows me the scribbled log.

Wonder how many invoices are paid late or never paid? This job is going to be a challenge. At least my other clients had accounting software and were trying to use it.

I must not be hiding my feelings very well because Logan's eyebrows draw together in a worried frown. "Noah, as you can tell, I need your help. Working on cars is what I love and what I'm good at." He points to the box. "This stuff, not so much."

I pull out the flyer with my service fees, but he waves me off. "I don't care what you charge. You'll end up saving me money in the long run, I'm sure."

We discuss payroll and how he pays his employees. He isn't keeping up with payroll taxes, so I need to get those paid as soon as possible. I describe my accounting software and how I can write checks or pay online via the software, with his approval.

Our discussion lasts about fifteen minutes. Logan isn't a dummy, he's just not knowledgeable about or interested in the financial side of his business. As I told Bob Robertson, this is why I started my company—to help guys like Logan.

He stands when someone yells for him from one of the service bays. "Sorry, but I need to get back to work. Do you need anything else?" He hands me the box.

"I'll email you a contract; please sign it as soon as possible and I'll get started."

"You're a lifesaver, Noah. I'm so grateful Darryl mentioned you to me." He smiles and starts to walk away. "Hey, if your vehicle ever needs service, it's on the house," he adds and strides away.

I pick up the box, knowing that it's going to take me several days to dig through all this and get everything organized. Chuckling, I think back to the weeks right after I got fired. It would be nice to have a little of that free time back again, but I wouldn't change how things worked out for the world.

Chapter Fifteen

Raelynn

I NEED ONE LAST CHRISTMAS gift for Mom. She mentioned a few months ago that she would like an authentic Red Wing crock for her front porch to put flowers in. So, I'm at Twice Again to see if they have one.

Twice Again is a fascinating store. Filled to the brim with eclectic secondhand items, you can find almost anything for anyone. In autumn, I noticed that the store was packed with tourists, so I avoided coming here until now.

A tall slender lady is working behind the checkout counter. I glance around looking for Noah's sister, Ellie, but she's nowhere in sight. Although Noah promised to more formally introduce me to his sister, between the holidays and his new business, he's been so busy that I haven't bugged him about doing so. I thought this little shopping trip would be a perfect opportunity to get to know Ellie better, so I'm disappointed when she's absent.

"May I help you?" the lady asks when I get within a few steps of the counter. She doesn't address me in an overly exuberant voice much like some salespeople do. In fact, I'd say her manner is somewhat standoffish.

"Is Ellie around?" This prickly young woman is giving off a vibe that says, "leave me alone." I'm surprised Margaret hired someone with this personality.

"She's at lunch," she says in a huffy voice. The woman glares at me as if I'm an inconvenience.

I notice her nametag reads Riley, so I try a friendlier approach. "Riley, I'm looking for a Red Wing crock for my mom. Do you have any?"

Her demeanor immediately goes from sour to sweet. "Yeah, we do. Follow me." We walk to the back of the store, where there's all different sizes of the white crocks.

"What are you going to do with it?" Riley asks.

"Mom wants to put it on her front porch and fill it with flowers."

Riley nods and digs through the stack, pulling out two crocks and holding them up for my inspection. "This is an antique one; you can see that it's a little weathered and there's a chip along the rim." She rotates the crock, around showing me the chip. "But the distinctive Red Wing mark on the front is still in good shape."

I take the crock from her and turn it around in my hands, looking at all sides. "It's quite heavy," I say.

She laughs. "They're made from clay and they're called stoneware for a reason. The company dates back to 1877 and was located in Red Wing, Minnesota."

"I didn't know that. Is this crock from 1877?" My voice rises with surprise.

Riley shakes her head. "No, those crocks were cobalt blue and are extremely rare. The one in your hand is probably from the 1920s. We'd have to research the mark to find out the exact date of production. The number indicates how many gallons the pot can hold." She points to the 5 on the front of the crock.

Riley really knows her stuff. She's impressed me with her knowledge. "I like this one. The chip and weathered mark give it character."

Riley smiles. "I agree. This other crock is a reproduction, and isn't worth as much either."

Looking closely at the vintage crock, I imagine all its owners over the years. It would be fascinating if it could talk and share its journey through time with me. "I'll take this one."

"Come up front and I'll ring you up."

When we get back to the front, Ellie walks in. She smiles and waves to me.

"Hello, stranger," I say. Since Noah now drops off and picks up Sofie, I never see her aunt anymore.

"It's been a while, hasn't it? Are you buying something?" She nods towards the counter where Riley is ringing up my purchase.

"A crock for mom for Christmas. Riley was extremely helpful."

Ellie smiles at her colleague and I see a slight blush on Riley's cheeks at the compliment. "There isn't much about antiques that Riley doesn't know." She turns back to me and says, "We need to get together for dinner sometime. I'll give you a call."

"I'd like that."

She nods. "I better get back to working on the table I'm refinishing in the back," Ellie says as she walks away.

"I hope your mom enjoys this," Riley says as she hands me a bulging bag with the pot inside. It's wrapped in a couple layers of newspaper, but I still don't dare drop it.

Thanking her, I leave, carrying the heavy bag with both hands. On the way home I ponder how I can get to know Ellie and Riley better.

Chapter Sixteen

Noah

I FOLD LIKE A HOUSE of cards under the pressure of a five-year-old. Yep. We're headed over to Frank's place to look at the puppies. I tell myself that we'll just "look" at them, but who am I kidding? *Let's just hope my daughter doesn't talk me into getting two.*

Turning onto the nondescript gravel road, my SUV bounces along much like last time. Sofie giggles in the backseat. "This road is bouncy." I suspect Frank likes it this way—it cuts down on the number of visitors.

When I pull up to the farmhouse, I notice a new front door painted a bright red color. *Frank's been fixing up the place a bit.* Sofie dances at my side as we climb the porch steps and knock. She's singing "puppies, puppies, puppies," in her sweet high-pitched voice. I think the tune is from a *Frozen* song, and she's been singing this for the last fifty miles. Repetition doesn't bother my daughter.

"Come in!" Frank says as he flings the door open, a welcoming smile on his face. We bustle inside, trying not to let too much of the cold air in. *Am I in the right house?* A new leather sofa and loveseat sit across from each other in the living room. Colorful pillows are tastefully arranged on each piece of furniture. This room is a far cry from my last visit with Rae. My brows draw together in confusion as to what's the cause of this new stylish look, then it hits me. *June.*

"I'm here to see the puppies," Sofie shouts while she removes her coat and deposits it on the floor. We have this discussion at home every day about her hanging up her clothes rather than dropping them all over the place. Obviously, my teaching is not having much impact. I lean down, retrieve the discarded coat, and hand it and mine to Frank.

"Looks like Miss Sofie is excited about seeing the puppies," Frank says with a wink as he hangs our coats in the entry closet. My daughter spins and twirls around the living room, all the while singing about the puppies. She bounces from the sofa to the loveseat, back and forth, like she's a ball in a pinball game.

"Guess you could say that," I reply dryly.

Frank laughs. "Well, let's go see them." He motions for us to follow him as he walks towards the back of the house. Sofie runs up to his side and takes his hand. I'm just along for the ride, I guess.

We enter what looks like a mudroom with a large cardboard box in the corner. The mother dog is lying down, and six puppies are crawling on top of and around her. Some puppies are all black, and some are a mixture of black and white.

Sofie shrieks in delight and puts her little hands over her mouth while she patiently waits for Frank to pick up one of the puppies. We had a long talk in the car about how to be gentle with little puppies. When he hands one to her, Sofie's face radiates pure joy. She sits down on the linoleum floor, cradling the puppy in her arms. I whip out my phone and take a picture of the endearing sight.

"He's so warm," Sofie says as the furry bundle squirms in her arms and tries to lick her chin.

"That one's a girl," Frank says. He looks at me and adds in a low voice, "Thought you might want a female."

I nod my agreement.

"Why are they in a box?" Sofie asks.

Frank chuckles. "It keeps them contained and close to their mama."

We play with the puppies for several minutes. I even get in on the action, holding one in my arms. I'm surprised Frank has any left, with how cute they are.

"A couple of them are already spoken for," he explains when he leaves two in the box and doesn't bring them out to meet us.

Sofie and I are absorbed in the puppies when a familiar voice from the doorway says, "Hello! I see you've met the puppies."

June is standing there, holding a couple grocery bags in her hands. Frank walks right over and relieves her of the bags. He kisses her cheek, and she blushes. "I'm fixing fried chicken for dinner. Noah, hope you and Sofie can stay."

"Fried chicken!" Sofie yells, sealing the deal that we'll be staying.

The adults laugh. "That's a yes, then?" June asks.

"Yes, but we didn't bring anything to offer to the meal," I reply.

"Oh shoo! I've got plenty of food. You play with the dogs and we'll have dinner ready in about an hour," June says. Frank and June go off to the kitchen, leaving us to play with the puppies.

I hear laughter and conversation in the kitchen. I've never seen Frank move so fast as he did when June arrived. I can't wait to tell Rae about Frank's new furniture and his kiss on June's cheek.

Some time later, the delicious aromas from the kitchen waft into the mudroom, making my stomach growl. Frank appears and says, "Dinner will be ready in a few minutes. Have you decided which puppy you want, Miss Sofie?"

She grins up at him. "I like these two. Can I get both of them, Daddy? Please?" Her eyes plead with me to say yes.

I can feel my resolve slipping, when luckily Frank intervenes, saying, "How about you choose one. Then if no one takes the other one, your dad can decide if you can have that one too?"

I chime in, adding my two cents. "Since we're new to having a dog, I think we should do as Frank says. Just take one for now."

Sofie looks heartbroken but doesn't complain. "Then I pick this one." She points to the chubby black and white one that's been her favorite for the last several minutes. I like that one too. The white under her chin and on the tip of her tail is unique. I nod.

"Okay, I'll save her for you. She'll be ready to leave her mom on Christmas Eve." Sofie squeals with delight.

Frank returns all the dogs to the box while my daughter and I wash our hands. When we enter the toasty warm kitchen, June has the table set and is dishing up mashed potatoes into a large bowl. Frank picks up the platter filled with fried chicken and sets it on the table. June hands him the potatoes and then pours hot gravy into a serving dish.

"Please sit, whatever seat you want is fine," Frank says.

"This looks and smells delicious," I say as Sofie and I take seats on one side of the table while Frank and June sit on the ends.

"Thank you, Noah," June says.

Sofie reaches for a wheat bun and puts it on her plate.

"Shall we pray?" June asks politely before any more food hits anyone's plate. She instructs us to all hold hands while she says the prayer. "Bless us, O Lord. We are thankful for these friends and your gifts, which we are about to receive from your bounty. Through Christ our Lord. Amen."

Frank says "Amen" in his deep voice and I follow suit. Sofie looks wide-eyed at the whole proceeding, but she chimes in with Amen in her sweet, high-pitched voice. Apparently I need to introduce prayer at our nightly dinners; that's a real oversight on my part.

The meal is appetizing and filling—I haven't had fried chicken for such a long time, I eat several pieces. Sofie even cleans her plate. June baked brownies for dessert, and we all manage to have room for one despite the big meal. Frank and I clean up while June and Sofie go back into the puppy room.

"So, you and June are getting serious?" I ask as I load the dishwasher.

He laughs. "I asked her to marry me and we're getting married on the Friday after New Year's."

My eyeballs almost fall out of my head. "Wow, that's fast."

"When you're my age, you don't beat around the bush. I asked June last week and she said yes." He beams. "She'll be calling you and Rae with an invite," he adds. *I have some serious updates to tell Rae about tonight!*

Once the kitchen cleanup is done and the ladies return from the mudroom, I tell Sofie it's time to leave. "Thank you for the delicious dinner," we say as we get our coats on. "We'll come and get the puppy in the morning on Christmas Eve."

Frank and June wave goodbye as we walk out to our car. Frank puts his arm around June, and they look like a happy married couple.

On the way home Sofie asks, "What does Amen mean?"

"That's an ending for a prayer. It means we all agree with what was said in the prayer."

"Oh."

"We'll start praying at every meal. How about that?"

Sofie nods. "I'll say Amen at the end."

~*~

"How did the puppy visit go?" Rae teases on our nightly call that evening.

I chuckle. "How do you think it went?"

She laughs. "You ended up getting two of them."

"Almost. But Frank intervened and told Sofie to pick one, and he'd let us know if the second one was still available."

Rae giggles. "Did you encourage Frank to make sure the second one gets adopted?"

"Um, well, no. Sounds like the puppies are pretty popular, so I don't think that will be an issue." My voice rises in excitement as I speak my next sentence. "You'll never guess who came while we were there."

"June?"

Rae told me several times there was a romance brewing between Frank and June, so I'm not actually surprised she guessed correctly.

I expel a disappointed breath. "You just took the wind out of my sails." Her uncontrolled laughter floats over the line, so I wait a few beats for her to compose herself. "And much to my amazement . . . Frank kissed June right in front of Sofie and me," I add with theatrical flair.

Rae gasps, letting me know I have her full attention now. I grin at how my next piece of juicy gossip is going to blow her away.

"Oh, it gets even better . . ." I pause for a few seconds, adding to the drama.

"Don't make me wait, Noah! Spill!"

I feel like beating a drum roll with my fingers for this big reveal. "Well . . . they're getting married the Friday after New Year's. June's going to call with an invite."

"This is so wonderful!" Rae squeals a lot like my five-year-old. "The stained-glass window project helped get them together."

Once hearing returns to my left ear, I also tell her about Frank's new front door and furniture. "Guess he had to spiff up the place for his fiancée."

"She's a good influence on him. They're perfect for each other," Rae says with a breathless sigh.

I want to say "we're perfect for each other too" but I don't. I need to be patient until May 23.

Chapter Seventeen

Raelynn

MY RED DRESS LOOKS FESTIVE, and I attach the sprig of holly brooch that Mom gave me to give it a final Christmasy touch. It was Grandma's pin, and I wear it every Christmas Eve. Grabbing my purse and coat, I head out to the service. Pastor Tim warned all the members to get to the church early because there's always an overflowing crowd on this holiday.

I take one of the last parking spots in the FaithBridge lot. Other attendees are going to have to park along the street. A friendly older gentleman hands me a program and a small candle, then directs me to the open pews at the back. Sofie waves enthusiastically at me as I walk over to join Noah and her.

"We saved you a seat," Noah says with a bright smile. He's looking handsome in a charcoal gray suit and red tie. I haven't seen him in a suit since our painful first meeting, so I notice how the jacket shows off his broad shoulders. A swarm of butterflies flutter in my stomach at the sight.

"I got a puppy!" Sofie announces in a loud voice as she hops up and down. Despite the organ music playing in the background, everyone in the pews next to us heard that announcement. Several people chuckle.

When I get settled in the pew, sitting between Noah and Sofie, I say, "When did you get a puppy?" I act surprised even though I knew about the planned trip to Frank's farm to get the fur baby.

Sofie claps her hands. "This morning! And she's so cute."

Noah gently reminds her to use her indoor voice.

"What's the puppy's name?" I ask in a whisper, hoping Sofie will take the hint.

"Stinky," Sofie says not using the indoor voice. "She made a big poopy mess and Daddy said she was stinky." The little girl then falls back into her seat in a fit of giggles.

"We're going to come up with a better name once we get to know the puppy better," Noah says firmly.

I nod. "I wouldn't want to be known as Stinky just because of one accident."

Sofie chews on her finger as she considers my words, then she shakes her head in agreement.

"What color is she? Maybe you can find inspiration for a name because of her color?" I suggest.

"She's black and white," Sofie replies.

I ponder names that might work with that color combination. *Pepper? Too boring. Inky? Too close to Icky. Spot? How unoriginal.* I keep all my mediocre name suggestions to myself.

Pastor Tim strides to the altar and the crowd settles down; conversations quiet when he says, "Thank you all for coming to this celebration of Christ's birth. We are also celebrating the restoration of our hundred-year-old stained-glass window." He points to the window, which looks glorious with the church's lights catching the different colors and making them glimmer. "I'd like the volunteers who restored the window to stand so we can thank them properly."

He informed us a few days ago that he would be making this announcement and asking us to stand. Noah and I stand first, then Sofie jumps up, hugging Noah's legs. Frank and June are seated a few pews up from us and they rise to their feet together. Frank looks like a million bucks in what appears to be a new suit while June beams beside him in a dark green dress. They are the cutest couple, and I can't wait to attend their wedding.

Someone in the front of the church starts clapping and soon everyone joins in. The noise fills the sanctuary as it reverberates around us. People turn in their seats to stare at us. As I look across the church, a sea of smiling faces meets my eyes. After what feels like several minutes, the crowd quiets back down, rotating back to face the front.

"Thank you, Frank, June, Noah, Rae, and little Sofie for all your time and effort. We'd like each of you to take one of the poinsettias home with you at the end of service." Pastor Tim nods to the beautiful red flowers lining the altar. I put my hand to my heart, touched at the unexpected gift. The emotional moment is broken when Sofie pipes up, "He mentioned me!" Noah looks embarrassed at the outburst, but the congregation chuckles as we sit back down.

"Please stand and join me in singing 'O Come All Ye Faithful,'" Pastor Tim says while the organ plays the introductory notes of the song. I blink back tears when the soaring organ notes and uplifting voices swell across the sanctuary in perfect harmony. Noah takes my hand, squeezes it, and doesn't release it until the song ends. Although I know we shouldn't hold hands in public, I reluctantly let go.

The rest of the service flies by. One of the extremely talented choir sopranos sings a solo of "O Holy Night." I see people across the sanctuary wiping tears away at the poignant rendition. After Pastor Tim's sermon retelling the birth of Christ, the church lights are dimmed, and ushers walk down each aisle, lighting the candle of the person on the end of the pew, who then lights their neighbor's.

Pastor Tim's words linger in the air as the light slowly moves across the sanctuary. "As John tells us in chapter eight, verse twelve, when Jesus spoke again to the people, He said, 'I am the light of the world. Whoever follows me will never walk in darkness, but will have the light of life.'"

Once all the candles are lit, we sing "Joy to the World." The stained-glass window depicting Jesus' birth looks ethereal in the flickering candlelight. After the last note is sung, the church lights come back on. I blink a few times at their brightness compared to the candlelight. We gently blow out our candles, collect our things, and get ready to depart. The crowd murmurs around us as they do the same.

"I officially joined FaithBridge," Noah says after the service is over.

I smile, wishing I could give him a hug. "Congratulations! I guess I'll be seeing you at Sunday services from now on."

He blushes. "We'll try to make the early service, but no guarantees." We both snicker, knowing that the little girl dancing between us is the reason for his statement. "Shall we get our poinsettias?" Noah asks as we exit the pew. I nod and follow him to the altar where Frank and June join us.

"Don't you look pretty," June says to a bouncing Sofie, who reiterates about getting the puppy.

"You and Frank make a lovely couple," I say to June in a low voice.

She blushes and says, "As do you and Noah."

Are we that transparent? We better tone it down or someone else is going to notice, and that wouldn't bode well.

Sofie skips over to Frank and pulls on his pants leg. He bends down and she says, "I love the puppy, Uncle Frank!" My eyes widen at the uncle comment.

Noah shrugs and whispers to me, "Frank said to call him uncle." I knew Frank was just a big softie behind that gruff exterior.

Frank looks touched at her comment. "I'm glad she has such a good home. I know you'll take good care of her, Sofie." The little girl nods solemnly.

We each take one of the potted red flowers and join the crowd exiting the church. Several people walk over and tell us how beautiful the window turned out. Their heartfelt gratitude makes all the hard work and late-night Saturdays worth it.

Pastor Tim greets every person on their way out of the church. This man could make even the most jaded person a believer. His good wishes and firm handshake fill you up with God's glory like an empty bucket left out in the rain. Whenever life throws me a curveball lately, I remember one of Pastor Tim's inspiring sermons or his hearty handshake, and it helps sustain me.

When I get to the exit, Pastor Tim takes my hands in both of his large, work-roughened hands. "Rae, you are a blessing, and I'm so glad you found our church. Have a Merry Christmas and enjoy the visit to your Mom's house." The man never forgets anything you tell him because I mentioned several weeks ago that I was spending Christmas Day with Mom. "Same to you, Pastor Tim. Thank you for the flower." I hold up the red plant grasped in my hand and he smiles then says a few words to Noah.

Noah and Sofie walk me to my car. It's as if we don't want to be separated yet on this special night. I pull out a small tin from my car and hand it to Sofie. "Merry Christmas."

She squeals and looks excitedly at her dad. He nods and she opens the tin to find the cutout sugar cookies I made last night. All different shapes, including Santa, Rudolph, the Christmas star, and a dog with a big red bow. I iced them and decorated them with lots of sprinkles. "These are so pretty!" Sofie exclaims. "Can I have one, Daddy?"

Noah chuckles. "Just one for now." She nods and selects a Rudolph, then dances around us as she eats it. Noah shakes his head at his daughter's antics, taking the tin from her before she spills it across the parking lot.

We gaze into each other's eyes for a few beats until Sofie runs into my legs, almost knocking me over. "Oops," she says by way of apology.

"I better get this one home so Santa can come," Noah says under his breath.

"Merry Christmas, and enjoy your meal with Ellie and Margaret tomorrow."

Noah laughs. "I'm fixing ham this time. No strange body parts to contend with," he says with a smirk. "Merry Christmas," Sofie and Noah shout and wave as they walk to their car.

I clutch the poinsettia to my chest, my heart overflowing with happiness as I gaze at the two most important people in my life. *Who would have guessed I'd fall in love with the parent of one of my students.*

Chapter Eighteen

Raelynn

THE HOLIDAYS ARE OVER AND school's back in session. With New Year's falling on a Tuesday, it makes for a short week (thankfully!).

Friday night is Frank and June's wedding. June explained that the wedding is on a Friday because the happy couple are flying off early Saturday morning to Germany to spend their honeymoon exploring Europe. Frank said he always wanted to go and what better time than the present? Frank sure is a changed person since meeting June.

"Hey," Cassie says as she plops down in the chair across from my desk, the only other adult-sized chair in the room. "Are you as tired as I am?" Her usually neat ponytail is sagging, and her shirt boasts a blue stain of unknown origin, although I suspect finger paint.

I nod and laugh. "Two weeks away from our students, and now we can't keep up with them." As I glance at her hair again, I'm grateful for my new shoulder-length cut; it's perfect for this job. Now rather than trying to keep my long hair in a ponytail or bun all day, I just comb it a few times and it's good as new.

My colleague exhales a loud breath. "My students were extra rambunctious today. Had to tell me all about their Christmas gifts. I didn't realize puppies are so popular for Christmas."

Laughing, I tell Cassie how excited Sofie was to tell Angela about her new puppy. "Sofie even made up a breed for her puppy when Angela bragged about hers being a Goldendoodle."

Cassie shakes her head in amusement. "What did she say it was?"

"A Farmdoodle!" It was hilarious. I had trouble keeping a straight face. "Wait until I tell Noah."

Cassie raises one of her perfectly manicured eyebrows. "You and Noah still a thing?"

A spike of worry hits, especially after June's innocent comment about Noah and me being a cute couple. *Who else has noticed?* "We're playing by the rules. No dating. Just nightly FaceTime calls."

"That man is handsome as the day is long." My colleague teasingly fans her face. "I bet you're counting down the days until end of school."

A blush heats my neck and cheeks. "Don't tell anyone, but I have a countdown calendar at home. I'm marking off each day with a red X until May 23."

Cassie high fives me. "You go, girl! Noah sounds like a great, upstanding guy, and you deserve a guy like that."

We chat for a little longer about our lesson plans for the next week. Principal Marshfield wants to hold a fundraiser in the spring, and Cassie and I are heading up the planning committee, so we also talk about that for a few minutes.

"It's going to be a busy spring," Cassie says as she departs.

~*~

The church is tastefully decorated with white ribbons at the end of every pew, a red runner down the aisle, and a candelabra of white candles flickering near the altar. I pause for a minute, taking in the breathtaking sight of the restored stained-glass window as it reflects the candlelight.

"Rae, how are you doing?" Pastor Tim says with a broad smile. "We're running with a small crew this evening, so there's no ushers. Do you mind directing people to their seats as they arrive?" He hands me a stack of the wedding programs and strides away.

I giggle. "Yes, I'll be happy to," I say to thin air.

After hanging my coat on the racks in the vestibule, I position myself at the back of the sanctuary so I can greet people as they arrive. *Is there a bride side and a groom side in terms of seating?*

Just as I'm pondering that question, Frank strides up from the front of the church. He again looks like a million bucks in that new dark gray suit. A red rose is pinned to his lapel, and he's sporting a new haircut.

"I heard you got recruited to greet our guests," he says with a chuckle.

"I guess you can call it that!" We both laugh, knowing how Pastor Tim operates.

"June said you'd be worried about which side to sit guests on?"

Trust June to think of everything. "Yeah, I was just thinking about that."

Frank faces to the front of the church and points. "Groom side on the left, bride side on the right. Sound okay?"

I nod.

"We're not expecting a very large crowd, so ask them to take the front-row pews first."

"I will." I glance at my watch and see that there's only fifteen minutes until the start of the wedding, so I expect people should start arriving soon.

Frank disappears just as an older couple I don't know walks in. I hand them a program and direct them to the correct side. The remaining minutes until the ceremony become a blur as more and more guests arrive. I think Frank underestimated how many people were going to attend. Knowing June, she probably invited the entire FaithBridge membership.

Noah and Sofie walk in with five minutes to spare. "I didn't know you were an usher," Noah teases.

Rolling my eyes, I say, "I'm a last-minute recruit."

Noah nods. "Ah, so Pastor Tim requested your help then?"

I suppress a snort. *No one can turn down the gregarious pastor.* "Save me a seat and I'll join you and Sofie once the ceremony starts."

"You look pretty, Miss Dailey," Sofie says shyly beside me.

I bend down to her level. "So do you, Sofie. Is this a new dress?" She's wearing a fancy pink dress with a tulle skirt. The only thing she forgot is her tiara.

She nods and chews on her thumb. "Daddy says I look like a princess."

Noah chuckles. "She's going through the princess stage," he whispers.

I don't tell the poor man that she's probably going to be in that stage for several more years. "The dress is gorgeous," I say as I hand him a program and he and Sofie take a seat on the less-populated groom's side.

More and more people arrive, keeping me busy. Conversations murmur around the church as people greet each other and take their seats. For a low-key affair, there sure is a great turnout.

The organist slides onto her bench and music flows across the sanctuary. I love the robust sound of a real pipe organ. When Pastor Tim walks to the altar, a hush descends over the crowd. He's soon joined by Frank and another man who looks a lot like him. *Maybe a brother?*

I slip into the pew beside Noah and Sofie. Sofie leans over and whispers, "This is my first wedding." The excitement in her voice is palpable. She puts her little hand in mine, and I squeeze her hand back.

Strains of the traditional wedding song fill the church. Every eye turns towards the back of the sanctuary. A pretty lady dressed in a blue knee-length dress walks down the aisle. She smiles and nods to guests on the bride's side, so I assume she's related to June. If I had to guess, I'd say she was her daughter.

The six-year-old granddaughter follows, spreading white rose petals along the red runner in the aisle. She's so cute in her matching blue dress, and there's several "awwws" as she proceeds down the aisle and joins her mom.

"I want to do that someday," Sofie whispers in my ear.

My heart flips in my chest as Sofie's words evoke an image of Noah's and my wedding. *You're getting ahead of yourself, Rae.*

When the organ swells, we all stand, and the blushing bride appears at the back of the church. June is wearing a gorgeous cream-colored knee-length dress. She's radiant and beaming as she walks down the aisle, her eyes never leaving Frank's. Her bouquet of red roses trembles in her hands. It must be her son who's walking with her. I get a tissue from my purse and wipe away tears at the touching sight.

Frank takes June's hand, and they join Pastor Tim at the altar. I've never seen Frank smile so broadly before. He looks like he just won the lottery.

"They look happy, don't they," Noah leans over and whispers as I continue to wipe the tears leaking from the corners of my eyes. I can only nod because emotion clogs my throat. He takes my hand, squeezes it, and we hold hands until the ceremony is over.

When Pastor Tim announces that Frank and June are husband and wife, the crowd claps and cheers—the raucous sound echoing around the church. Much to my surprise, Frank plants a big kiss on June's lips, causing the crowd to cheer even louder.

Pastor Tim instructs the guests to join the happy couple in the coffee serving area off to the side of the church. June had informed me they were serving cake and light snacks.

We walk through the receiving line, where Frank gives me and Sofie a big bear hug. Noah and he exchange handshakes.

June squeals and hugs me tighter than Frank did. "I'm so glad you could come," she says.

"It was a beautiful wedding, June. And you're a gorgeous bride," I say as I return her hug.

June pulls Sofie into the hug and the three of us laugh and hug for several beats. She beams and smiles while Frank looks adoringly at her. "Sofie, you need to meet my granddaughter sometime," she says before we walk away.

Everyone sits at the long tables, enjoying the cake and what turns out to be finger sandwiches. Laughter and joy flow across the guests. This is a blessed celebration, and I'm so happy Frank and June found each other. I'd like to think that Noah and I played a small role in their romance by recruiting them both to work on the stained-glass window.

"Sofie, I forgot to ask you, what did you name the puppy?" Hopefully Noah talked her out of the Stinky moniker.

She licks icing off her fingers, then replies. "Frankie. After Uncle Frank," she says matter-of-factly.

My heart warms at the appropriate name. I mouth "perfect" to Noah and he smiles.

"When are you and Miss Dailey getting married, Daddy?"

Noah's mouth drops open in surprise. "We haven't even gone on a date, Sofie."

I smirk internally knowing that I thought about our wedding not more than fifteen minutes ago myself.

She shrugs her little shoulders. "You look at Miss Dailey just like Uncle Frank looks at Miss June."

Is that true?

Both Noah and I look around to see if anyone heard that proclamation, but everyone is too busy eating and talking to pay any attention to us. When Noah catches my eye, we both gaze at each other like two lovesick teenagers.

Out of the mouth of babes.

Just this morning I counted the number of days until May 23. One hundred and forty days and counting. Can my heart wait that long?

Chapter Nineteen
Noah

TODAY'S BEEN A LONG DAY. I can't believe how quickly January flew by and now it's February. Colorado weather can be unpredictable this time of year. Temperatures are in the sixties one day, and the next day, fifteen inches of snow covers the ground. The meteorologists are predicting just such a snowstorm later this week, so I'm making hay while the sun shines, as they say. Visiting each of my clients to kick off the start of tax preparation season.

After my busy day, I barely make it in time to pick up Sofie. Rushing in, I join the throng of parents retrieving their offspring. Rae and I do our usual polite, school-appropriate greeting while Sofie collects her things and I bustle her off to the car. Now that Sofie blurted out about how I gaze longingly at Rae, I've been trying to keep a more neutral expression when I see Rae at school. We're absolutely playing by the rules, so I wouldn't want anyone, especially Principal Marshfield, to get the wrong idea.

"I thought we'd pick up your favorite fast food tonight," I tell Sofie after buckling her into her seat in the back. I need to organize everything while the tax discussions with my clients are fresh in my mind, so tonight's going to be a late one and I don't have time to cook.

Sofie claps at the mention of fast food. "Can I have a kiddie meal?"

"Sure. And we're both having a side salad instead of fries." My New Year's resolution to eat healthier hasn't been shattered yet.

Sofie wrinkles her nose. "Fries are better, Daddy."

We go through the drive-thru and I stay resolute about getting the side salads even though the fries smell delicious. I swear this place pumps that odor into the air so everyone within a five-mile radius is drawn in for the fried potatoes.

Sofie sings to the radio on the way home. The country station plays wholesome songs for the most part, and I don't mind Sofie singing to them. Some girl's twangy voice is singing about all the things she knows how to do that a man ought to know how to do. The tune is catchy, and I'm all right with Sofie getting the message that women can catch a fish or change a tire at the side of a road. The song ends right as we pull into the driveway.

"Who's that lady, Daddy?" Sofie asks the minute we turn in.

A woman dressed in a bright pink poufy jacket paces on the front porch. When she looks up, my heart drops like a rock to my toes.

"Here, you play this game on my iPad while I go talk to her," I say in a rush before the woman can approach the vehicle. After handing Sofie the tablet, I scramble out of the SUV, leaving it running so Sofie doesn't get cold. She's strapped into her car seat, so there's no chance she can get into any trouble.

"I was wondering if you were ever coming home," my ex-wife says in an annoyed voice as I join her on the porch.

"What are you doing here, Victoria?" My voice doesn't sound friendly, just as I intended.

Her eyes narrow as she looks me over. Then she points to my SUV. "Sofie sure has gotten big." Sofie stares at my interchange with Victoria. She obviously doesn't recognize her mom because she hasn't seen her since she was three months old. "When did you move?" Vicki adds.

Coldness drips from my lips. "Sofie and I downsized a few months ago . . . Why are you here?" I repeat in the same unfriendly tone.

She gives me a puzzled look at the downsizing comment, her finely groomed brows drawing together. Vicki loved the other

120

house. She talked endlessly about remodeling this and that, always wanting the latest home finishes. *Vicki always valued things over people.*

"I want to reestablish a relationship with my daughter."

My mouth falls open in shock. *Didn't she give up that right when she left us without a word and I got custody?* My memory is kind of fuzzy about what exactly happened. It was an emotional time for me, but my attorney will know the details.

"Look, Noah. I've changed. I regret leaving you and Sofie. I want to work out a visitation schedule with my daughter that works for both of us." Vicki holds out her hands in a pleading motion.

I blow out the breath I've been holding. "I'm not sure how comfortable I feel with a visitation schedule." My calm words belie how my heart is almost pounding out of my chest in panic at the mere thought.

"I'm her mother," Victoria says quietly. "I've grown up these past few years. I'm begging you, Noah, to not turn me away."

My mind scrambles with how to handle this situation. Not in a million years did I think I would come home today to find my ex-wife standing on the front porch. "Now isn't a good time. How about we meet tomorrow at a coffee shop after I drop Sofie off at school?" I say reluctantly, buying me some time to formulate a plan.

She nods and I give her directions to Sacred Grounds. Before I turn to go back to my vehicle, Victoria squeezes my arm. "Thank you, Noah."

Conflicting feelings swirl around inside me like a pack of angry hornets. *How can she reappear after five years and insist she be part of Sofie's life?* I jump back in the car while Victoria watches me pull into the garage.

"Who was that lady, Daddy?" Sofie says as she watches Vicki walk down the sidewalk and out of sight.

"A lady from Daddy's work," I reply. I don't want to tell my daughter it was her mother.

~*~

I've got no hope of focusing on work this evening. Victoria's reappearance is too emotionally distracting. I barely manage to choke down my double cheeseburger. After the discussion with Vicki, I wish I'd gotten the fries.

I don't mention the encounter any further, and Sofie seems to have accepted my story. In any other instance I wouldn't lie to my daughter, but I don't know how this situation is going to play out, so I justify the falsehood in my mind.

Once Sofie's tucked into bed and we've read her bedtime story, she nods off quickly. I tiptoe out her door, softly clicking it shut. Once I'm in my bedroom behind closed doors, I dial Rae.

"I thought you were working late. I didn't expect to hear from you," Rae says in her cheery voice.

"Me too. But I had an unexpected visitor when I got home."

"Oh? Who?" I hear papers shuffling as Rae does something on her end of the phone.

"My ex-wife. Sofie's mother."

The paper noise stops abruptly. After several beats, Rae says, "What did she want?" There's a tinge of concern in her voice.

I exhale loudly. "She wants to establish a visitation schedule with Sofie."

Rae gasps. "That's a big ask. I thought she signed away her parental rights after she left?

I told Rae bits and pieces about Victoria leaving, but not everything.

"When I think back, I'm not sure that she signed away her rights but rather gave me full custody . . ." My voice trails off in fear that her case for getting any visitation rights isn't as impossible as I hope. "Victoria claims that she's changed and wants to reestablish a relationship with her daughter. I have a meeting tomorrow morning at eight with my attorney to see what rights Vicki has in this case. Then I'm talking to Vicki at eleven."

"Oh, Noah. You must be feeling so conflicted." Rae's supportive tone makes me feel marginally better.

"I never told you the whole sad story, Rae. I'm not blameless in this mess."

I hear a chair squeak as Rae sits down. "Tell me everything, Noah."

I sigh loudly and launch into the story. "Sofie was a colicky baby. She rarely slept through the night. Since I was the one working, Vicki agreed to get up with Sofie every night." I remember those days as if it were just yesterday.

"As the weeks wore on, I could tell it was having a physical impact on Vicki. She was fatigued and irritable all the time and sometimes fell asleep right after dinner. She'd break into crying jags for no apparent reason. Vicki was immature and not mentally prepared to take care of a newborn. Before she had the baby, Vicki even admitted she wasn't ready to be tied down. She wanted to go out with friends at the drop of a hat, and that was much more difficult once Sofie arrived."

I pause, thinking of all the dumb mistakes we both made. "Now that I know more, I think Vicki also had some form of postpartum depression."

A small, sympathetic "oh" comes across the line, followed by, "Did she get any help at the time?"

"When I suggested that, she said it was just temporary and she refused to see a doctor. Unfortunately, looking back, I think she was ashamed of the feelings she was having . . . One time she handed me Sofie and said, 'I can't deal with her anymore' and just left the house. She was gone for six hours and I never knew where she went."

Retelling the story is difficult even now. I pause and take a sip of water, then continue. "Vicki had good and bad days. I never knew which Vicki I'd come home to. I hate to admit it, but I was absorbed in my job and didn't pay much attention to the signs that Vicki was going to leave. I should have recognized it; she'd left me one time without explanation back when we were dating. Her immature and selfish behavior surprised me when she came back and laughed about the fact that she ran off with some friends to Vegas without even letting me know. I worried about her all weekend, and she just ignored all my texts and calls."

I shift on the bed where I'm sitting, trying to get more comfortable. "When Sofie was almost three months old, I came home and a neighbor was watching Sofie. I was shocked and annoyed at Vicki for just leaving our child without letting me know. And it was so much worse."

The memory still makes me quite angry, so I pause a second or two to calm down. "That was the last time I saw Vicki in person except for today. Two months after she disappeared, her attorney and my attorney worked everything out—Vicki filed for divorce, ending our marriage, and I got full custody of Sofie."

"That time must have been really hard for you. How did you cope?" The sadness and empathy in Rae's voice almost do me in.

I groan. "Not very well. I wish I'd known Pastor Tim, because he would have been a good person to turn to. Ellie had just broken up with her long-term boyfriend, so after Vicki left, she came to live with us, and I began living as if my career was the only important thing. I thought if I could make a lot of money, I could make up for having been a bad husband to Vicki . . . I failed her and Sofie." The honest admission makes me sag in relief.

Rae sniffles. "Noah, you shouldn't blame yourself. This is your chance to forgive Vicki. Let your past transgressions go. I suggest you talk to Pastor Tim after you talk to your attorney. He can help you open your heart to God for guidance."

I exhale a loud frustrated breath and make a confession. "Right after I saw Vicki, I asked myself why God would let this happen. Sofie and I are so happy. Why did Vicki come back into our life?" I feel guilty about these thoughts, yet I share them with Rae.

"You're only human, Noah. Your faith can carry you through this. Think about Vicki's side of things. If you made a mistake, would you never want to be allowed to see your daughter again?"

I shake my head at Rae's wisdom and unfailing faith in God's path for us. *How did I get so blessed to have her in my life?*

"I'll call Pastor Tim tomorrow." Just the mere suggestion makes me feel better.

"I'm praying for you, Noah," Rae says quietly. "Call me anytime if you need to talk. Even if you wake up at two in the morning and need to talk, I'm here."

"Thank you, Rae, you're a wonderful friend." I want to tell her that I'm falling in love with her, but now is not the time.

As I climb into bed, I say a prayer asking for guidance. *God, please help me know what to do and what's best for Sofie.*

Chapter Twenty
Noah

AFTER A RESTLESS NIGHT WITH little to no sleep, I drag myself out of bed, trying to act like everything is normal, for Sofie's sake. As I watch my little girl cheerfully eat her cereal, my heart almost breaks in two. She chatters to one of her stuffed animals and pretends to feed it. Her blonde curls bob around her shoulders; her happy giggles warm my heart. She's precious, beautiful, and the light of my life.

"Daddy, you look sad. Are you having a bad day?" Sofie asks between bites of her favorite breakfast cereal.

I plaster on a fake smile. "No, just thinking about my busy day. We better get you off to school." She nods.

When I drop Sofie off, Rae is manning the drop-off area today. She waves and mouths, "I'm thinking about you." I smile and wave back as if I don't have a care in the world.

Jesper Anderson has been my attorney since Victoria left. He knows my case inside and out. My spirits rise as I drive into the familiar lot and walk into the red brick building. My attorney will know the best course of action, I'm sure.

"Noah, please sit down," Jesper greets me warmly. He's a tall thin gentleman, and he's looked the same ever since I met him.

We shake hands and I sit in the chair he indicates. He sits back down at his massive desk, perches a pair of reading glasses on his nose, and opens a thick folder, glancing down at the contents. My left leg wants to bounce up and down to expel my nervous energy, but I put my hand on it to hold it in check.

"So, your ex-wife wants to reestablish a relationship with your daughter, if I understand it correctly."

"Yes, she showed up out of the blue yesterday asking to see Sofie."

Jesper peers at me over his glasses. "As you know, you have full custody of your daughter. But your wife did not sign away her parental rights. At the time, you decided not to push for that," my attorney says as he reads through papers in the file. "It was an emotional time, Noah. If I remember correctly, you just wanted the whole mess to be over. Once you had custody and the divorce was final, you chose not to take it any further."

I shift in my seat, remembering the details better. "What visitation rights does she have?" I croak out, my throat clogged with fear.

Jesper removes his reading glasses and looks straight at me. "Noah, I don't think you want this to go to court. Although you've been an outstanding father to Sofie, the court may grant Victoria partial custody. If she can prove she's changed, has a stable job and living situation, the court will look on that favorably. In my experience, the court tries to reunite parents with their children, whenever possible."

I lean forward in my chair and pinch the bridge of my nose. "What do you suggest?" I say in a defeated voice.

"Talk to Victoria, get a feel for her situation. See what you can work out with her. It's fairly easy to change the custody agreement—we would simply petition the court for a modification, adding visitation rights for her, or whatever you agree to. If you or Victoria object to the modification, things get much more legally complicated and we'd have to go to court."

My chest feels like I've been stabbed in the heart. The pain of the reality that I've got to let Victoria back into Sofie's life almost paralyzes me. I want to scream or cry or pound my fist on the desk—but instead I sit here impassive, holding all my emotions in.

"I'm here when you need me, Noah. Go talk to Victoria and then let me know what I need to do."

Minutes later, I'm sitting in my car in the parking lot. A feeling of despair washes over me, much like how I felt months ago when I lost my job. But unlike in that situation, I have people I can turn to now. Pulling out my cell, I call Pastor Tim. His wise counsel will help me put things into perspective.

"This is Noah," I say once the pastor answers.

"Noah! How can I help you?" Just hearing his booming voice makes me feel better.

I have to clear my throat twice before I can ask, "Do you have time to talk right now?"

"Yes, I'll meet you in my office at the church in half an hour," Pastor Tim replies, concern lacing his voice.

~*~

The pastor's office is a cramped space with a desk, two guest chairs, and a couple bookshelves filled with books of all shapes and sizes. The Bible lays open on top of the desk, its dog-eared pages revealing how much he uses it. Passages are highlighted in yellow.

Once we're seated, the pastor steeples his fingers under his chin. "Noah, how can I help?"

His stare is intense yet friendly. He gives off the vibe that he can help solve anything. He's that rare personality—a combination of charisma, faith, and empathy without coming across as being arrogant or judgmental. He exudes confidence, thus making you feel more confident in the process.

"My ex-wife showed up yesterday and wants visitation rights with Sofie. She hasn't seen her daughter since Sofie was three months old . . . I'm struggling with what to do." My voice cracks with emotion.

Pastor Tim leans forward in his chair. "That is difficult." His sympathetic expression is all the encouragement I need to tell him everything.

I talk for several minutes about how Victoria just up and left. How I petitioned the court and got sole custody. I also tell Pastor Tim about what my attorney said—that I would probably lose if I attempted to fight Victoria on visitation rights. "I want to do what's best for Sofie," I say as I shake my head in frustration. "I want to believe that Victoria has changed, but I don't know if I trust her."

The minister thoughtfully nods, absorbing everything I told him. "Have you forgiven Victoria for leaving you and Sofie?"

My eyes widen. *Have I forgiven her?* I was bitter when she left, and even more so during the divorce. But should I deny my daughter getting to know her mother because *I can't forgive*?

The pastor picks up his Bible and thumbs to another page. "Ephesians 4:32 tells us 'Be kind to one another, tenderhearted, forgiving one another, as God in Christ forgave you.'" He looks back up. "My advice, Noah, is to forgive your ex-wife and then ask God to guide you with your decision. Without forgiveness, your mind will be clouded. Forgiveness will free you to see things in a different light."

I let the pastor's word sink in. What he's asking feels impossible, so I feel compelled to explain my part in this mess. "I wasn't blameless in this, as I mentioned—"

The pastor interrupts, "Then maybe you also need to forgive yourself."

We talk a little longer, and I start to feel the burden of blame for my failed marriage and the guilt for not helping Victoria when she needed it being lifted from my shoulders. By the time I leave the pastor's office, I have faith that God will guide me and help me through this.

"Noah, I will pray for you. If you need to talk again, just reach out."

As I drive away, I thank God that he put Pastor Tim in my life.

~*~

Victoria is already at Sacred Grounds by the time I get there. The irony of the coffeeshop's name is not lost on me.

"Thank you for meeting me," she says as I join her at the table carrying my cup of coffee. She grips her cup so tightly that her knuckles are white, giving me a hint that she's also nervous about this conversation.

"I'd like to work this out amicably. The last thing Sofie needs is her parents fighting over her."

Vicki nods. "Yes, I agree."

"Are you planning on moving back to Paradise Springs? How would the visitation work?"

She clears her throat. "I just got a new job in Trinity, and I'm planning on moving in with a girlfriend." *I wonder whether this new job will stick since she bounced around from job to job before we got married.*

I raise an eyebrow, not sure I'm comfortable with adding a stranger to the mix. Vicki holds up her hand. "Before you pass judgement, I'm not suggesting overnight visits right now. I'd like to visit Sofie here for a while. Take her to the park or a playground or out to lunch. She and I need to spend some time together, get to know each other."

Her plan sounds reasonable. It appears that my ex-wife has grown up and matured. "I'd like to be at the first visits. I don't want Sofie to feel like she's being left with a stranger."

"Absolutely. I don't want to traumatize our daughter."

We discuss the details of Victoria meeting Sofie this upcoming Saturday afternoon. Vicki will come to the house. I'll ask Ellie to be

130

there as well. We can all eat dinner together if everything works out.

When I stand to leave, Vicki says, "Noah, one of my greatest regrets was leaving you and Sofie. I wish I had gotten medical help for how I was feeling. I'm sorry, and I hope you and Sofie can forgive me."

"I'm working on it," I grumble, then stride out of the coffeeshop.

~*~

I feel like I'm flying blind. How do you introduce a five-year-old to the mother she hasn't known since she was three months old? I've consulted several books on the topic, read scores of blog posts, and have prayed every night for guidance. Everything I read suggests that I talk to Sofie about her mom and then introduce the idea of meeting her mom prior to the actual meetup.

We're eating breakfast the next day and I broach the subject. Since Sofie saw the lady on the porch, first I need to be honest about who that was.

"Sofie, you remember how we've talked about your mom, right?"

She nods her head as she continues to spoon cereal into her mouth.

Needing more than just a head nod, I try again. "What do you remember?"

"My mom left when I was little. She went to live in a different city."

When Vicki left, she moved to Denver, so I had explained that to Sofie. "That's right. How would you feel about meeting her?"

Sofie's eyes widen, and a beaming smile lights her face. "She wants to meet me?"

Her instant excitement almost breaks my heart. Although I'm reluctant to show any excitement, I force myself to be upbeat. "Yes, very much. The lady on the porch a few days ago is your mom."

Sofie scrunches up her face, as if she's trying to conjure up a picture of what her mom looks like. "She's pretty and has hair like me."

My heart warms at how smart Sofie is. "Yes, she has blonde hair like you. I talked to her yesterday and she wants to meet you on Saturday, here at the house."

"Will you be here?" Sofie sounds a little panicked.

My heart swells knowing that my presence is all it takes to make Sofie feel safe and secure. "Yes, and Aunt Ellie's going to be here, too. We'll fix dinner for your mom and we'll all eat together. How does that sound?"

"Can we have spaghetti?" Sofie asks excitedly.

I chuckle. "Yes, you can help Aunt Ellie and me plan the menu."

"I want chocolate milk too."

I shake my head in amazement as to how resilient this kid is. She doesn't seem at all concerned about why her mom's been missing all this time, and I hope she doesn't ask.

~*~

A five-year-old asks a lot of questions. I've been answering questions all week about Mommy. Some I can answer and some I cannot.

"What's her name?" Victoria.

"Does she have a puppy?" I don't know, but we'll ask her on Saturday.

"Where does she live?" Trinity.

132

I pulled up a map on the iPad and showed Sofie where that town is in relation to Paradise Springs. Turns out it's about a forty-minute drive away.

"Does she like macaroni and cheese?" I don't know.

But macaroni and cheese has been added to the menu, just in case her mom likes it.

"Can we watch *Frozen* with her?" Yes.

I think Vicki should experience watching this film a million times, so why not start now?

Surprisingly, the questions about why her mom left and why she hasn't visited until now have not come up. I'm sure these tough questions will come up eventually, but I'm going to let Vicki answer them.

Bright and early Saturday morning, Sofie is up and ready to meet her mom. I slowly crack open an eye, and the clock on my nightstand reads 5:30 AM.

Sofie bounces on my bed. "Daddy! Time to get up. Mommy's coming over today."

Groaning, I roll over and give my daughter a stink eye. She just giggles.

"What do you want for breakfast?" I say as I yawn and get out of bed.

"Pancakes!"

Of course she doesn't want something simple like cereal today. I plaster on a smile and say, "Pancakes it is."

After breakfast we "clean" the house. This involves picking up the living room and Sofie's room, both of which have clothes and toys scattered about. Sofie grumbles about doing it, but when I tell her that Mommy will want to see her room, the grumbling magically disappears.

Ellie comes over for lunch and we start on dinner preparations. With all the fuss both females are making, you'd think we were preparing for a visit from the Queen of England. Sofie has a meltdown when she learns that we don't have chocolate milk. I make an emergency run to the grocery store to get some.

Five o'clock finally comes. I'm exhausted and cranky because of all the drama over the food. Did we make enough spaghetti? What if Mommy doesn't like green beans? Should we fix a salad? Let's try a fancier recipe for the mac and cheese . . . The list goes on and on as we all fret over the meal. At least we can't change the menu again at this point.

Vicki arrives fashionably late. At least that's what I tell Sofie. Twenty minutes may not seem much to Vicki, but it is to a five-year-old.

"Sorry I'm late! There was an accident on the highway, and we were stopped for forever," Vicki says in explanation. I usher her in while Sofie hides behind me and Ellie hovers in the living room. I sequestered Frankie in the laundry room because I remembered my ex-wife doesn't like dogs. *We don't need Vicki to reject Sofie's pet on her first visit.*

Vicki smiles at Sofie as I pull my daughter out from behind my legs. Sofie's chewing on her finger, which she does when she's nervous. Vicki bends down and extends her hand. "I'm your mom and I'm so excited to meet you." There's an awkward few seconds while Sofie looks Vicki over from head to toe, but she finally extends her hand and they shake. My daughter then looks up at me for guidance.

"Shall we sit in the living room until dinner's ready?" I ask.

Ellie comes forward and shakes Vicki's hand. "Nice to see you again, Vicki." Even though she says the right words, they don't come out in a very friendly tone.

Vicki ignores it. "Nice to see you too, Ellie."

Ellie, me, and Sofie sit on the couch while Vicki takes the loveseat. Sofie snuggles into my side and continues to chew on her finger. *What are we going to talk about?*

Thankfully, Vicki keeps the conversation going. "I like this smaller house. It's very cozy. And you've decorated it so well."

I point to my sister. "Ellie works at a refurbished furniture store and I got everything there."

"Oh? I should go there. What's the name of the store?"

"Twice Again," Ellie replies in a cold voice.

Silence. The conversation lags as we all look uncomfortably at each other. Sofie finally saves the day.

"Wanna see my room? I have an Elsa and Olaf blanket," she says excitedly.

"That would be wonderful!" Vicki says as she hops to her feet. She extends her hand and Sofie takes it, leading her mother down the hall. Mother and daughter chat about Sofie's room as they walk ahead of us.

"Well, that was awkward," Ellie says under her breath as we follow them.

The bedroom tour goes well. Ellie disappears to check on dinner while I linger at the doorway. Sofie shows her mom the *Frozen* bedspread, her toys, her books, and even some of her dresses. Once Sofie gets going, she's unstoppable. Vicki oohs and aahs over everything and truly seems interested. Although she's playing the mom role well, I wonder whether the immature, selfish Vicki will reappear. A twinge of guilt hits at even thinking those thoughts.

It's a relief when Ellie calls us to eat. Sofie's warmed up to her mom now and is the one handling all the conversation, excitedly telling Vicki about the menu. I give Vicki credit; she says all the right things. It gives me optimism that Vicki's desire to see her daughter is genuine and that she's in this for the long haul.

"I love this mac and cheese. Where'd you get the recipe?" Vicki directs the question to Ellie and me.

"The internet," Ellie replies curtly.

Trying to smooth things over, I say, "Sofie wanted it to be extra special."

Vicki smiles and turns to Sofie. "This whole meal is extra special."

Sofie beams. "Do you like the chocolate milk?"

Vicki picks up her still full glass of milk and chugs some down. I can tell by her expression that milk isn't her favorite beverage. "I never have chocolate milk, so this is a rare treat."

My ex-wife is really trying, and I appreciate the effort. She's winning Sofie over completely, and even me to some extent. Ellie is going to be more difficult to come around.

"We're having chocolate ice cream with sprinkles for dessert!" Sofie adds.

"I can't wait," her mom says.

The visit ends after we've stuffed ourselves and cleared the dishes.

"This has been wonderful, but I need to get home," Vicki says after her offer to help load the dishwasher was turned down. Ellie insists on cleaning the kitchen and shoos us out.

Sofie and I walk Vicki to the front door. She bends down, and Sofie hugs her this time rather than a handshake. "Can you come back next weekend? We can have chocolate milk again!" Sofie says excitedly.

Vicki looks up at me for guidance. "I'll talk to Mommy and we'll plan something that works with all our schedules," I reply.

Returning her daughter's hug, Vicki says, "I can't wait to see you again, Sofie." She then puts on her coat and mouths "thank you" to me.

Once Vicki is gone, Sofie grabs my hand and dances beside me. "Mommy is nice! Can she move in with us?"

My eyes widen at the suggestion, but I expected questions like this would arise. "Mommy has her own house in another town."

Sofie looks crestfallen.

"But she can come visit again. Maybe we can go to the park next time if it's warm enough."

Sofie nods and skips off to the kitchen, asking Ellie for more chocolate milk.

I hope the subject of Mommy moving in doesn't come up again, but somehow, I expect it will. Rae's pretty face pops into my head. Isn't it ironic that the person I'd actually love to have over for dinner tonight is Rae, and yet I can't do so until after May 23?

Chapter Twenty-One
Raelynn

THE SPRING SCHOOL FUNDRAISER IS only a few weeks away, and our little planning committee is meeting today. I thought we had plenty of time to plan this event, but where did February go? The blustery weather reminds me of the saying "March comes in like a lion and out like a lamb." Today is definitely lion weather.

A few weeks ago, I called for help from Twice Again when fundraiser donations started pouring in and we had nowhere to house them and no idea how to price them. Margaret wisely appointed Ellie and Riley to assist Cassie and me, realizing that the task was going to take a large chunk of time. They're both already sitting at a booth at Sacred Grounds when we arrive. I'm excited for this chance to get to know them both better.

"It's freezing out there! Where's spring?" I complain as Cassie and I plop down in the booth across from Ellie and Riley. We're both wearing our winter parkas, with gloves and scarves.

"Tell me about it. My daffodils are under a foot of snow," Cassie adds.

"Yet we had sixty-degree temperatures a week ago," Riley says, confusion over the fickle weather on her face.

Ellie bellows out a laugh. "Welcome to Colorado!" We all join in the laughter.

After we retrieve our coffee orders from the serving bar, the informal planning committee meeting begins.

"All the donations have been cleaned and are ready to display on the silent auction tables," Ellie says.

"We received fifty donated items, and Margaret donated another ten items from the store, so we have a good selection. The grand prize is from Twice Again—an old-fashioned rocking chair like the ones they have at the Hitching Post restaurant," Riley reads from a list on her laptop.

The group 'oohs' over the grand prize.

"Did we get good stuff or just junk?" Cassie asks.

Riley and Ellie exchange a look. "Some of each. But, as you know, one person's junk is another person's treasure," Riley says with a smirk.

"Let's hope we have lots of treasure seekers at the auction," I say, and everyone nods.

"Did you set minimum bids on everything yet?" Cassie asks the antiques experts.

"Most things. Ellie and I are conferring with Margaret on a couple items we weren't sure about, but we'll have those done next week," Riley says, still referring to her laptop.

"Where did you learn so much about antiques?" I've been curious about Riley's background since she helped me select the crock for Mom.

She shrugs. "My grandmother raised me, and everything in her house was an antique."

My eyes widen. I'm sure there's a lot more to that story but Riley quickly changes the subject. "Are we setting up the night before? Ellie and I will need to pack everything and move it to the school gymnasium." They're storing everything at Twice Again until the auction.

"I'll recruit some parents to help," I say.

"Preferably parents with big muscles," Cassie says while showing off her biceps.

"I'll ask Noah to help," Ellie adds with a wink directed at me. Cassie volunteers her current boyfriend to help as well, although at the rate she goes through boyfriends, he might not be around in two weeks.

I draw up a schedule for setting up the silent auction and then a schedule for who's going to work at the tables. Someone will be at the tables at all times during the bidding session to answer questions and encourage bids. Once the bidding closes, Cassie and I will announce the winners. Ellie and Riley will process payments for the auctioned off items. Margaret has graciously offered her credit card payment equipment for those who want to pay that way.

Once all the details are hashed out, we chat and enjoy refills on our coffee. Cassie orders a plate of scones, which we all hungrily tear into. The warm cinnamon and raisin pastries are delicious.

"How's Noah and the ex-wife?" Cassie says. We've been too busy with school to talk lately.

I shrug. "He's been spending a lot of time with her, helping Sofie get to know her mother." I try not to let disappointment leak through my voice. While I'm happy for Sofie, this new arrangement puts a damper my nightly calls with Noah. Seems like Noah's consumed by meetups with Victoria so she and Sofie have time together. Noah always accompanies his daughter since she isn't completely comfortable with her mom yet—and he reluctantly admitted that he isn't fully comfortable with his ex-wife yet either.

"Vicki's been a little demanding, and Noah bends to her every whim. He's scared she'll petition the court for partial custody, so he's trying not to rock the boat," Ellie explains.

I nod in understanding, even though I wish he wasn't so amendable to every one of his ex-wife's demands.

"Is he considering getting back together with her? Wouldn't that make things a lot simpler for everyone?" Riley asks.

An awkward silence greets her words. Riley doesn't know about my relationship with Noah and Sofie, so she doesn't realize how she stuck her foot in her mouth. She looks around the table at our surprised looks. "Hey, I'm just saying. My experience with men is they always take the easy way out."

Would Noah do that? Get back together with his ex-wife?

Ellie vigorously shakes her head. "Noah has no desire to rekindle a relationship with Vicki. He just wants Sofie to be happy."

After the meeting breaks up, Riley's words stick with me all night, running around in my head, creating seeds of doubt. *Would Noah get back together with his ex-wife? Is my relationship with Noah over before it even gets started?*

Chapter Twenty-Two
Noah

THIS IS SOFIE'S FIRST TIME to stay overnight at her mother's house. The mother and daughter have had several weeks to get to know each other, with Vicki coming to Paradise Springs for all those visits. Last weekend Vicki took Sofie to the park by herself, and everything went well even though Sofie begged me to go along. I politely declined despite Sofie's pouty face.

I knew it was inevitable that Vicki would want Sofie to visit at her house, but I'm not ready for it. Worry knots in my stomach, and I feel like my daughter's moving out rather than just going away for one night.

Yesterday I notified the school that Vicki will be picking up Sofie today after school. The plan is for Sofie to stay with Vicki tonight and then tomorrow until around noon, when I'll come pick her up. Since tomorrow's Saturday, neither Vicki nor I need to work. I'm glad that Vicki's roommate is gone for the weekend; one less person for Sofie to adjust to.

Sofie and I eat breakfast together like we always do. She seems extra fidgety, but I chalk that up to excitement.

"Do you have everything in your bag?" I ask while Sofie and I examine the contents of the bag together. We had to move to a larger suitcase when it became evident that three stuffed animals and two dolls must accompany Sofie on this trip.

My daughter runs over to her bookcase and pulls out three books. "Can I take these too?" Frankie tracks her every move as if she knows that her favorite person is going somewhere.

I chuckle. "Yes, sweet pea, you can take those stories." I cram them in the already overloaded pink suitcase. You'd think Sofie was packing for a week rather than one night.

"Show Mommy your bag before you unpack so she knows everything that needs to come back home with you." Although I can't imagine Vicki has any kid supplies at her house to get things confused with.

Sofie nods, then flits off to find another pair of socks to take along. "I need these!" she squeals when I try to talk her out of bringing a third pair of fuzzy pink socks, so I give in and the socks go into the suitcase.

I grab her coat and school backpack and head out to the car. Groaning dramatically, I lift the suitcase and put it into the trunk. "Do you have rocks in here?" I tease. Sofie giggles.

On the drive to school, Sofie chatters about the overnight adventure. "Mommy said she got me a new bed," Sofie tells me for the twentieth time. "And it's got an Elsa blanket!" Even though she has a Frozen comforter at home featuring Elsa, Anna, and Olaf, I guess she can't get enough of the Disney characters.

When I drop Sofie off at school, I reiterate with Rae that Vicki is picking up Sofie this afternoon. "I'll watch for her," Rae says with a thumbs up as she stores Sofie's suitcase in a locker. My worry makes me sound like a mother hen, but I don't care.

The day flies by with several client meetings, and by the time I get home it's dinnertime. Frankie greets me at the front door, sniffs my legs, and gives me a confused look. "Sofie went to visit her mom," I say lamely. Frankie lifts her doggie eyebrows, then turns around and trots to her poufy bed in the mudroom. Apparently, I'm too boring.

After five minutes, the quiet house seems far too empty and too quiet without Sofie chattering a mile a minute about what she wants to eat. I fill a glass with water and the clock in the kitchen starts to annoy me. *Tick tock, tick tock.* When did it start ticking so loudly?

All week I told myself that tonight will be "Noah time." I can watch anything I want on TV, I can eat anything I want, and I can go to bed as late as I want because I won't have a five-year-old to wake me up at 6:00 a.m.

After only an hour, I'm bored stiff, so I order a pizza just to interact with the delivery kid.

"It's cold for March, isn't it?" I say as the teenage delivery guy hands me the pizza box. He looks at me quizzically at my lame attempt to strike up a conversation with anyone, even a stranger half my age. After I give him a big tip, he says, "Thanks, man!" and sprints down the front porch to his car as if he can't wait to leave.

When I wander back into the kitchen, the silence is overwhelming. *Tick tock, tick tock.* I quickly backtrack and eat in front of the TV, watching a show about dragonflies that I'm sure Sofie would love. Did you know there are over 5,000 known species of dragonflies? *I'll make sure to tell Sofie that tomorrow.*

Around eight, my phone rings with Vicki's name lighting up the screen. My heartrate leaps. *Did something happen to Sofie?*

"Hey, what's up?" I try to modulate my voice so I don't sound worried, but I don't do a particularly good job of it.

"Your daughter wants to speak to you," Vicki says with a huff. *That doesn't bode well.*

"Daddy, I want to sleep in my own bed," Sofie says in a small voice between sniffles.

I sit up straighter on the couch. "Okay. Want me to come get you, sweet pea?"

When she doesn't answer, I suspect that she's nodding. She always forgets people can't see her over the phone.

"Let me talk to Mommy."

There's a muffled noise at the other end as the phone is handed over. "Do you want me to come get her?"

"Yes," Vicki says in a defeated voice. "I guess I rushed things. Sofie got scared when it got dark outside. And then she didn't like the bed because it's too big. And the room's too dark." Vicki exhales loudly.

"It's okay. She wasn't ready yet." I try to keep the gloating out of my voice. At least I manage not to say I told you so. "I'll be there as soon as I can."

"Thanks, Noah."

I change from my "Noah time" ratty sweats and baggy T-shirt to blue jeans and a Henley shirt. Grabbing a warm jacket, my keys, and wallet, I jog out to my SUV.

The drive to Trinity takes forty-five minutes on a good day, but I make it in thirty-five. When I pull up to Vicki's house, all the lights are on. After I knock, a disheveled Vicki answers the door and motions for me to come inside. Sofie rushes over and clings to my legs as if she never wants to let go. I gently rub her head as I speak with Vicki. "Is this everything?" I ask when she hands me the suitcase.

"Yeah, Sofie decided she didn't want to unpack, so it's not been touched." Vicki looks like she's on the brink of tears, making me feel sorry for her.

"Hey, we'll try this again another time," I say in a low voice. Vicki nods.

"Say goodbye to Mommy," I say as I nudge Sofie to disentangle herself from me.

She detaches herself from my legs long enough to wave and whisper, "Bye." I help get her coat on and we walk hand in hand to the SUV. After buckling Sofie into her seat, I hop in the front and drive away.

On the way home Sofie says, "Daddy, I don't want to go anywhere without you ever again."

Her words warm my heart because I missed her so much in the few hours she was gone. "Didn't you have fun with Mommy?"

She shakes her head. "It was too scary without you. I'm sorry." Her little lips tremble and a tear slides down her cheek.

Her sad expression makes my heart ache. "Sofie, you don't have to be sorry. And you don't have to go anywhere without me again. I promise." I'm sure she won't feel this way in ten years, but for now I'm happy to be her person—the safe haven she needs.

A small smile lights up her face and she chews on her finger. "Why can't Mommy come live with us?"

The question hangs in the air, and I hesitate to answer it knowing my daughter won't like the answer. When one of her favorite country songs comes on the radio, Sofie becomes distracted and we both sing to it. The happy sounds fill the SUV.

How do I explain why Mommy can't come live with us? I can't tell Sofie I no longer love her mom and that I'm in love with her kindergarten teacher. The thought hits me like a punch—*I'm in love with Rae.*

Chapter Twenty-Three
Raelynn

NOAH MUST HAVE HAD A busy weekend because he didn't call me for our nightly chat. Since the ex-wife entered the picture, our chats have been hit and miss. I want to be an understanding friend to Noah, but after meeting the gorgeous Vicki my confidence in our relationship took a big hit.

Sofie is the most important person in Noah's life. Would he get back together with his ex-wife just for the sake of his daughter? Doubts swirl, leaving me feeling unsure about my relationship with Noah that hasn't even had an opportunity to blossom.

Cassie waltzes into my classroom bright and early on Monday morning. She and I didn't have a chance to talk on Friday, so I know what's coming.

"What did you think of the ex-wife?" she says as she squeezes her tall frame into one of the small classroom chairs since one of my kid's rather overweight parent broke the leg off our only adult-sized chair.

"She's very striking—tall, blonde, and gorgeous," I say with a sigh. "Frankly, Cassie, I wonder how I compete." Once I saw Vicki, her appearance just added to my self-doubt.

My friend shakes her head. "You have nothing to worry about."

I bite my lower lip, but the truth spurts from my mouth. "Noah didn't call me at all this weekend. He's so preoccupied with the ex-wife lately. I'm a second thought at best."

Cassie's eyes widen. "Well, he was taken by surprise by this turn of events. Give him a little time to adjust, Rae."

I nod, knowing that I need to be patient and understanding, but the green-eyed monster wants to rear its ugly head.

"You'll see him next week at the silent auction. He's helping set up, right?"

"Yeah, as far as I know he's still helping."

She stands and gives me a hug. "Hang in there. I know everything will turn out. Remember, May 23 is just around the corner!"

My countdown calendar showed fifty-five days until May 23 as of this morning. *Will the ex-wife win Noah back before that and May 23 won't even matter?*

~*~

I call Noah on Tuesday evening after not hearing from him on Monday night either. My poor heart can't take any more waiting. The phone rings and rings, but he finally picks up.

"Rae, I'm so sorry I haven't called. It's been one thing after the other. I feel like all I do is fight fires."

His friendly voice is encouraging. Maybe I'm just being paranoid, letting all these doubts creep in. "What are all the fires?" I ask, trying to sound teasing.

He sighs. "First fire was on Friday night. Vicki called around eight for me to come get Sofie. She got scared and didn't want to spend the night." *Well that explains why he didn't call me that night.* "Then all weekend, Sofie wouldn't let me out of her sight."

My heart goes out to the little girl and the frazzled dad. I really was worrying about nothing.

He blows out another loud sigh. "She even had a nightmare on Saturday night about not being able to find me. I feel so guilty being part of the cause for her trauma . . . Plus with this being tax season, I'm scrambling to try to get my client's returns prepared and filed."

Poor Noah! I shouldn't be adding to his stress levels. "Noah, you shouldn't feel guilty. You're just trying to do what's right for

Sofie," I say in a comforting tone. I had noticed Sofie wasn't her usual perky self yesterday. She didn't talk about the visit to her mother's house at all, where the week before, that's all she could talk about.

He lets out a frustrated groan. "Between Vicki and Sofie being upset about the visit, I'm caught in between. I want to protect Sofie while at the same time help her get to know her mother."

"I'm no expert, but you might want to consult a child psychologist. Get their advice and help."

There's a pause and I hear him close a door in the background. "I will. Ellie has a friend whose child goes to one, so I'm going to contact her to see if she recommends the doctor, and then make an appointment."

Not knowing how else I can help him, I try to make my voice as sympathetic as possible. "I'm sorry you're going through all this Noah. I hope you know you can always talk to me when you need a friend."

"Thank you, Rae. I wish we had another project to work on together without breaking the rules. At least I'd see you more than five minutes when I drop off or pick up Sofie."

I smile, remembering all our fun working on the stained-glass windows. "You're still helping with the silent auction setup, right? I'll see you then."

He laughs. "You just want me for my muscles."

"I'll never admit to that! See you Friday night for setup."

After he signs off, I feel marginally better.

~*~

Tomorrow's the fundraiser, and we're all scurrying around getting everything prepared. The school gymnasium has been transformed into a spring theme with cutouts of tulips and daffodils adorning the drab walls. Long tables, where the silent auction offerings will be displayed, are just waiting to be filled.

Noah, Ellie, and several other parents arrive with the load of auction pieces from Twice Again. I direct them to start filling up the tables and I check off my list as they unload each item. Once everything is unloaded, Noah motions for me to follow him. We walk to the other side of the room so we can talk privately away from prying ears.

"Looks like a great assortment of items," Noah says as he points to the tables.

"Yeah, I'm excited with the variety. We should raise a lot of money."

"Sofie's been talking about this all week. That's why I wanted to speak to you privately," Noah says.

My eyes widen wondering what could be up. "Okay?"

"Sofie's invited Vicki to come to this. I wanted to make sure you had a heads up."

My heart plummets. I was looking forward to spending the day with Noah and Sofie, especially the dinner for all the volunteers once the auction is over. We hired several food trucks, and I was excited to see Sofie's reaction to the eclectic foods. And, of course, to spend time with Noah.

I'm trying to be supportive of Sofie re-connecting with her mom, but it's causing the relationship with Noah to slip further and further away. Plastering on a fake smile and keeping my voice upbeat, I say, "That's nice that her mother can attend. How are things going after the failed overnight visit?"

A small grimace crosses Noah's face, but he quickly hides it. *What did that mean?* "All is forgotten and forgiven with the overnight visit. Vicki hasn't pushed to try that again and Sofie seems content to have her mother visit here."

I try to read between the lines. Does this mean that Noah and Vicki are reconnecting as well since it appears that Noah is always present at these "visits"?

Noah's cell phone rings and he quickly answers it. I try not to listen in on his conversation but can't help myself. After a few seconds, he hangs up. "Sorry, but I need to go pick up Sofie. She's at a playdate with one of her friends—you know her, she's at Angela's house."

I silently blow out the breath I was holding, thinking that Vicki was at Noah's house watching Sofie. "Oh, that's great! Those two got over their crayon disagreement and are now fast friends."

Noah chuckles. "Sorry I can't stick around to help more. See you tomorrow."

I watch the attractive six-foot man disappear with a sinking feeling that my relationship with him is soon to be over.

~*~

The turnout for the silent auction is phenomenal. Looks like all the parents are here, and we've also got great attendance from others in the community. Ellie and Riley are chatting up the potential bidders as they walk around the tables. There's a lot of interest in the grand prize rocking chair, plus several of the other pieces. I just hope we don't have any items that don't receive even a single bid.

Noah, Sofie, and Vicki walk in about an hour into auction. Sofie's in the middle, and they're each holding one of her hands. It looks like the perfect family scene. I almost look away, but Noah draws my gaze in his blue jeans and flannel shirt. The outfit plus the sexy scruff on his cheeks makes him look like a hunky mountain man.

Vicki's dressed to the nines in black figure-hugging pants and what looks like an expensive cashmere sweater, the blue color perfectly matching the color of her eyes. I feel like a country bumpkin in my newer blue jeans and casual pink Henley. Since I'm one of the workers, I wore this outfit for comfort, but now I wish I'd dressed up a bit more.

Sofie spies me and waves, causing them to walk towards me. "Welcome to the auction," I say in an overly enthusiastic voice. Hopefully, my fake smile hides the fact that my heart is breaking in two at the happy sight before me.

"Miss Dailey, this is my Mommy!" Sofie shouts while hopping up and down, her blonde curls bouncing around her shoulders. I notice that her hair color matches her mother's.

I extend my hand to Vicki. "We met one time before. I'm Sofie's teacher. Nice to see you again."

Vicki smiles and gives me a cool handshake, her smile not quite meeting her eyes. *What's that about?* Noah seems oblivious to the bad vibes coming off his ex-wife.

"Please look around and bid on whatever catches your eye. The highest bid wins, and bids are open until noon." My nervousness loosens my lips and I add, "And don't forget to enter the cornhole tournament for a chance to win two dinners from Jose's Tacos. Our school choir is performing in thirty minutes, and after that Principal Marshfield will take requests on her dulcimer from the audience."

I swear Vicki rolls her eyes as I ramble on about all the exciting activities other than the silent auction, especially when I mention the dulcimer. *I've been told that the principal is a very talented player and personally I can't wait to hear her.*

Sofie points to the grand prize rocking chair and drags her mom with her to look at it. Noah hangs back for a few seconds. "I don't want to upset their fragile relationship right now. Thanks for being understanding, Rae."

I nod, emotion clogging my throat. Noah's gaze locks with mine and I think he's going to say something more, but when Sofie

152

calls for her dad, he jogs away. Vicki says something and squeezes Noah's arm while they all laugh. They walk around, examining other items, and any observer would think they were husband and wife accompanied by their daughter. My heart crumbles and I furiously blink back tears. Fortunately, Cassie calls me over to the other side of the room, so I pull myself together and join her.

The large crowd keeps Cassie and me busy for the rest of the event. At least I don't have time to stew about Noah. We ring a bell at five minutes to go in the auction, encouraging any last bidders. There's a rush back to the tables by those last-minute lookers.

At noon, Cassie and I collect the bidding sheets and start calling off the highest bidders to come pay and claim their items. There's oohs and aahs as the winners are called. When we get to the final item, the rocking chair, my eyes almost fall out of my head. Noah is the highest bidder at $1,000. *Wow, that's an extravagant bid.* But his business is doing well and Noah likes to give back.

I call his name and watch as Sofie and Vicki clap. After he pays and collects the chair, I hear Vicki say, "Thank you! That's going to look great on my front porch." Cassie can't help but hear the exchange, and she gives me a sympathetic look. *He bought the chair for his ex-wife?* I hear the final nail being pounded into the coffin of my relationship with Noah.

Chapter Twenty-Four
Noah

I SAW THE LOOK ON Rae's face when Vicki blurted out that I bought the chair for her. Truth is, I didn't need a rocking chair, Vicki wanted it, and it was for a good cause. My feelings of guilt over the heartbroken look on Rae's face make me wish I'd never purchased it. I guess I didn't think things through—how it looked for me to buy something for my ex-wife. Afterwards, Ellie told me in no uncertain terms that I'm an idiot. *How do I fix this major blunder?*

As a fun Easter present, Vicki's going to take Sofie on an all-day excursion to the Denver Zoo on Saturday—just the two of them. This is my chance to talk to Rae and try to explain, tell her that I still have feelings for her. Ellie says that I need to grovel with flowers which hopefully doesn't violate Principal Marshfield's draconian rules. My spies (aka Cassie and Ellie) tell me that Rae is spending Saturday at home alone, with no plans, so I decide to surprise her by showing up at her door.

Sofie's talked about the zoo trip all week. I took her there last summer and she's extremely excited to go back. There were baby hippos at our last visit and Sofie wants to see them again.

My phone rings late on Friday afternoon. I just got home from Evans Garage and picking up Logan's latest box of papers. I can't talk the guy into doing anything on the computer, so we're still exchanging papers back and forth. When I see Vicki's name light up the screen, I swipe and answer.

"Hello, what's up?" I wasn't expecting to hear from her again until Saturday.

"Noah, I just got a terrific opportunity to accompany my boss to one of our premier clients. We're leaving on the first flight out of

Denver tomorrow, so I'm going to have to cancel the zoo trip with Sofie."

My heart skitters to a stop. *Sofie's going to be crushed about this.* "Can't you go on Monday? Sofie's been looking forward to this for two weeks."

Vicki expels a loud huff. "I knew you wouldn't understand. This is a huge career boost for me. I need to show my boss that I'm flexible and that my career is my top priority."

I pinch the bridge of my nose. The true Vicki is finally showing her stripes. She isn't ready to do the day-to-day heavy lifting of being a parent. If it's convenient for her schedule, she'll make time for Sofie. But Vicki's career takes highest priority, above her daughter.

I cringe, remembering that was also me just a few months ago. *Poor Sofie.* "You need to break this news to Sofie yourself. She'll be home from school in a few hours and I'll have her call you."

Silence greets my suggestion. After several long beats Vicki says, "Noah, I need to pack and get ready for the flight tomorrow. I don't have time to deal with Sofie. I'm sure you can break the news to her gently. Tell her we'll reschedule for another time." When the line goes dead, I stare at the blank screen in frustration. This is exactly why I had reservations about letting Vicki into Sofie's life— is she committed to our daughter or not? And now I'm the bearer of bad news.

When I pick Sofie up at school, Rae gives me the cool shoulder that she's given me all week. She's pleasant in a professional way, no cute grins or playful winks. With the zoo trip delayed, when am I going to fix the relationship with her? My heart sinks knowing I can't execute the "groveling" plan on Saturday.

Sofie chatters nonstop about the zoo visit on the ride home, adding to my feelings of frustration and guilt. I decide to tell her about Vicki backing out once we're home rather than risk a tantrum in the car, so I change the subject. "What was your art project today?"

I watch in the rearview mirror, and Sofie smiles. "We made a caterpillar. I can bring him home on Monday. He's green with yellow legs."

"Wow, he sounds cute."

Sofie giggles. "Caterpillars aren't cute, Daddy." She goes on to tell me all the facts she learned about caterpillars. My heart swells with pride as to how smart and engaged in learning she is.

After the dinner plates are empty and we're still sitting at the table together, I finally get the nerve to tell Sofie the bad news. "Your mom called this afternoon and she's not going to be able to go to the zoo on Saturday."

Sofie's face crumples. "Why not?" she wails.

"Mommy has to go on a trip for her job. She's sorry and she'll take you to the zoo another time." I'm not doing a particularly good job at selling this to my daughter because my heart isn't in it.

Tears stream down her face. "I want to see the baby hippos," she says in a disappointed high-pitched voice. Her lips tremble and she sulks. "They'll be grown up if we can't go!"

She has a good point—I don't want those baby hippos to be full grown the next time she sees them. I cave faster than you can say *hippopotamus* after I see the tears on my daughter's face. "How about you and I go to the zoo on Saturday instead?"

She sniffles and wipes her eyes, carefully considering my suggestion. "Okay," she says in a small voice.

"I heard they just had some baby gorillas a few months ago."

Her eyes go wide, and she claps with excitement, her tears drying instantly. "Yay! Baby gorillas." *It's amazing how quickly kids flit from emotion to emotion.*

We clear the dishes together while Sofie sings a song about baby gorillas, all disappointment about Vicki backing out forgotten.

But I haven't forgotten it, and I grapple internally with how to handle future visit requests from Mommy. Rae and Pastor Tim both suggested that to move on, I need to forgive Vicki. But, when she does something like this, it's difficult to do so.

After Sofie is tucked snugly into bed, a Plan B for the groveling with Rae hits me like a switch going on in my head. *When God closes a door, he opens a window.*

A smile crosses my face as I swipe my cell phone and place a call. "June, how are you?"

"Doing well, Noah. How can I help you?"

"Would you and Frank like to take your granddaughter to the Denver Zoo tomorrow? Sofie and I are going, and I thought the girls could meet each other."

June laughs. "What a lovely plan! When should we meet you there?"

"Actually, I need you to invite someone else to go along with you . . ."

My Plan B evolves to groveling plus cute baby gorillas. Hope it works.

~*~

Sofie is a bundle of energy and excitement the next morning on the drive over to Denver. We stop and have pancakes at her favorite breakfast restaurant. I'm really pulling out all the stops to make this trip special for her. The disappointment of Vicki backing out of the excursion is forgotten. I don't know what parenting books would say about how I handled the situation, but if my child is happy, I'm happy.

We're blessed with a warm spring day—the blue sky is stunning against the snow-capped mountains and the surrounding valleys that are just turning green. God's paintbrush has painted a breathtaking landscape.

The zoo isn't busy when we arrive. I scan the check-in area for Frank and June but don't see them yet. I dawdle at our designated meeting place by picking up the various zoo brochures under the pretense of reading them. Sofie's occupied watching two kids and their mom pay their entrance fees. I wonder if that scene highlights the fact that her mom isn't with us.

"Noah!"

I turn at the familiar voice. June, Frank, and the granddaughter approach. June waves while the granddaughter skips beside the other member of their group. My heart leaps at how beautiful Rae is both inside and out. She's smiling down at the granddaughter, and it lights up her face. Her outfit of blue jeans and a red sweater is simple and understated—exactly the look I love on her.

When Rae notices me, her steps slow and her smile falters. June says something to her, and they continue. By the look on Rae's face, she isn't happy to see me.

Sofie sees the group and tugs on my hand, pulling me towards them. "Look Daddy! It's Uncle Frank, Miss June, and Miss Dailey!" she says in an elated voice.

When we get close enough for introductions, June pulls her granddaughter forward.

"Sofie, this is Emily, my granddaughter. She's looking forward to touring the zoo with you."

The two girls shyly look at each other. After a few beats Sofie says, "They have baby hippos."

Emily looks at her grandmother and squeals with delight. "I love hippos!"

The ice is broken, and the girls chatter with each other as the adults walk back to the check-in area to pay. Frank and June chase after the girls when they run off following a peacock. I take the opportunity to pull Rae aside for a private conversation.

"I asked June to invite you so we could spend the day together. With Frank and June along as chaperones, we aren't really breaking the rules." The words tumble out of my mouth in a rush. "And I want to explain the situation with Vicki."

Rae stops and crosses her arms over her chest, staring intently at me. "You could have just called me."

I nervously shift back and forth on my feet. Rae's body language and glare aren't giving me much confidence. "I was afraid you wouldn't pick up. Please spend the day with me and Sofie. I'll answer any questions you have about my ex-wife and me."

She nods, but her cool expression doesn't change.

Sofie skips up after the peacock runs away; she tugs on Rae's hand. "Miss Dailey, they have baby hippos and baby gorillas!"

Rae shakes her head in amusement and grins. "Well, we need to see those."

When we get to the check-in counter, I pay for everyone, despite grumblings from Frank, June, and Rae. "My treat," I say in a firm voice.

The girls lead our little tour group as we follow the paved paths to the animals. I hang back and walk beside Rae. "I'm so happy you're here. I feel like I've made a mess of our relationship lately."

She gives me a side-eye glare. "You sure surprised me when you purchased that rocking chair for Vicki."

I stop and motion Rae towards a bench at the side of the walkway. The kids, along with Frank and June, are absorbed in the giraffe exhibit, so we have time to talk alone. "I got caught up in the auction, I guess. I wasn't thinking. Buying that chair for Vicki was a big mistake. It wasn't like I thought of it as a gift. I was thinking more about the donation to the school . . . I'm sorry if I hurt you, that was definitely not my intent."

Rae's eyes narrow as she thinks about my explanation. Then she sighs. "I jumped to conclusions. All I could see that day was a happy family—you, Vicki, and Sofie . . . and I wasn't part of it."

It never occurred to me how Vicki and I appeared that day to an outsider. "I've been too wrapped up in kowtowing to Vicki, afraid that she'll take Sofie away from me," I admit to Rae, my voice laced with regret and embarrassment. "My feelings towards you haven't changed, Rae. I'm still counting down the days to May 23."

She cracks a small smile. "Me too." Her eyes turn serious. "I understand your reluctance to stand up to Vicki, but at some point, she either has visitation rights or she doesn't. You can't always live in fear of what will happen next."

I nod and exhale a loud breath. "Vicki just added to my confusion. She backed out of this trip with Sofie at the last minute yesterday. Just the two of them were going and Sofie was so excited." I shake my head in frustration. "Vicki prioritized her career above her daughter." My throat clogs with emotion. "I brought Sofie here because she was so disappointed. How many times will Vicki disappoint her daughter in the future?"

Rae gently puts her hand on my arm. "I'm sorry, Noah. You have some tough decisions to make. Pray for God's guidance; He will help you."

This woman is so strong in her faith, she amazes me. My faith is like a rickety boat being tossed about in the rough ocean. Rae's faith is like a massive cargo ship cutting through the waves, strong and steady against the choppy waters.

The group yells at us that they're continuing with the tour. I stand and extend my hand to Rae. "Shall we enjoy the day and see where it takes us?"

Rae smiles and takes my hand. "We're breaking the rules left and right." She nods to our joined hands. I reluctantly let go and walk beside her. "I'll play by the rules until May 23, but no longer."

She giggles as we walk to catch up with Frank and June. "Come see the baby gorillas!" Sofie yells loud enough to be heard across the whole zoo. The adults laugh at the tiny girl's antics.

"Ellie told me to beg you for forgiveness. If I grovel at your feet by the baby gorillas, will you forgive me?"

Rae rolls her eyes. "Maybe, but only if you buy me one of those pretzels, too." She points to a red cart displaying freshly baked giant pretzels.

"Deal," I say.

~*~

We're eating lunch after seeing the baby gorillas and hippos. Frank and June are sitting side-by-side on the picnic table bench; a cozy sight as they share bites of each other's food.

"How was the honeymoon trip to Germany?" I ask.

June gives Frank an intimate look as a blush stains her cheeks. "We had an absolutely lovely time," she says. "Frank has relatives in Germany, and I got to meet them. That was a highlight of the trip." Frank smiles and nods, agreeing with whatever his new bride says.

I hear Rae chuckle under her breath beside me—the two lovebirds oblivious to anyone except each other. I wink at Rae, and she puts her hand over her mouth to keep the laughter inside.

Sofie and Emily eat their grilled cheese sandwiches and ask to go play on the kiddie playset beside the eating pavilion. "Stay where we can see you," I yell as they run away.

"The girls get on famously, don't they?" June says. "We should plan playdates for them more often."

I nod. "Let's do that."

"How's the puppy?" Frank asks in his gruff voice.

I'm surprised Sofie hasn't talked his leg off about the dog, but she's been too distracted by all the zoo animals. "Sofie loves that puppy. She named her Frankie after you." I swear I see a blush on Frank's neck when he hears that. "If we have a playdate for the girls at a park, we'll bring Frankie," I add.

The girls shriek with joy as they climb on the playset. Frank and June excuse themselves and walk over closer to the playground to watch the girls. Once Frank and June are out of earshot, Rae leans over and says, "Aren't they just the cutest couple. Look, they're holding hands." She nods her head towards the couple.

"Glad they found each other," I say.

Rae nods and grins. "I'm so proud that we had a little bit to do with their romance since we pulled them both into the stained-glass window project."

I laugh. "Believe whatever you want, Miss Matchmaker."

We clean up our trash and walk towards the play area. "Are you and Sofie coming to Easter service tomorrow? I've missed seeing you at church."

I grimace at our repeated absence. "I'm embarrassed to admit that since Vicki entered our lives, going to church has been a bit spotty." When I utter the words, I realize I've been avoiding the one place that can help me, acting as a balm to my soul. Who could leave one of Pastor Tim's sermons feeling down?

Rae raises her eyebrows, waiting for a commitment from me about tomorrow.

"We'll attend. Save us a seat."

Smiling, Rae says, "I'll see you bright and early. Tomorrow is sunrise service at 6:00 a.m." I groan and she laughs. "You won't regret going, Noah. Sunrise service is one of my favorites."

We join the rest of our group and a warm feeling flows through my body at my repaired relationship with Rae. *Will Vicki throw another wrench in it?*

Chapter Twenty-Five
Raelynn

NOAH SLIDES INTO THE PEW beside me just as the choir sings the first strains of "Christ the Lord Is Risen Today." The organ notes soar and the voices fill the sanctuary, causing me to blink back tears. Sofie sleepily waves at me from her perch on her dad's shoulder—her eyelids droop and she looks like she could nod off at any second. Little tremors zip up my spine as I gaze at Noah in his gray suit and red tie. He looks so handsome and debonair, a far cry from yesterday's mountain man. But I must admit, I love both looks.

He takes my hand, resting our joined hands on the seat between us, hopefully inconspicuous to the remainder of the congregation. His warm hand makes me feel happy and protected. I convince myself that I'll just hold on until the end of the song, but after the last notes are sung, I can't pull away. Noah squeezes my fingers as if he knows exactly what I'm thinking.

Today the altar is ringed with pots of white Easter lilies, in different color containers of pastel blues, pinks, and yellows. It looks like spring exploded around the raised platform. Pastor Tim assumes his position behind the lectern, greeting everyone in his booming voice. "He is risen!"

The audience responds with an equally loud "He is risen indeed!" making Sofie jump. Noah gently rubs her back, and she nods off again on his shoulder.

The sermon is a traditional Easter sermon, filled with hope and joy. About halfway through, the sunrise beams through the restored stained-glass windows, bathing the sanctuary in vibrant shades of the colors in the glass—yellow, green, blue, and orange.

It's a breathtaking sight, and several murmured "aahs" echo across the congregation.

Noah leans over and whispers, "It's like God is smiling down on us."

I blink at him with tears of happiness and joy in my eyes. Pastor Tim even pauses for a few seconds, letting the audience bask in the stunning sunrise reflected through the windows, because words can't really describe the sight.

When the sermon ends, everyone slowly trickles out of the pews, talking in small groups about Pastor Tim's poignant message. When Noah asks, "Did you enjoy the service?" all I can do is nod as emotion fills my throat. Being here with Noah and Sofie is like a dream come true. It makes me believe that everything will work out with Noah and me. For the first time in weeks, I feel confident in a bright future with the two people standing beside me.

We inch towards the exit doors; the line moves slowly because Pastor Tim says something to every person. "Would you like to join Ellie, Margaret, Sofie, and me for Easter dinner at my house?" Noah asks. "I'm baking a ham, Ellie's bringing scalloped potatoes, and Margaret is bringing dessert, although she wasn't specific as to what it is."

"Coconut bird's nest cake," Sofie says between yawns.

When Noah meets my eyes, we both chuckle. "How did you know that, sweet pea?" Noah asks.

"She told me," Sofie replies. "It's her special Easter cake."

"How could I refuse, with such a delectable menu?" I say, a broad smile on my face.

Noah leans over and says under his breath, "Don't feel pressure to come if you think it's breaking the rules."

I squeeze his arm. "I'm just having dinner with my friends."

His eyes go wide at my unexpected response since I've been so strict about "the rules," then he smiles, his eyes crinkling at the corners.

"What can I bring?"

"You and your bright smile," Noah replies with a wink.

"Noah, Sofie, and Raelynn, so glad you could come. May the Lord be with you," Pastor Tim says when we finally get to the front of the line. "The stained-glass window was resplendent, wasn't it? I thank God every day for your help restoring it." He gives us each a hearty handshake. I see Noah blinking back tears at the pastor's generous praise.

Before I get in my car, Noah says, "Thank you for inviting us. I needed your encouragement to get here, and I'm so glad Sofie and I came."

I nod. "Hopefully, you'll be able to join me from now on."

He laughs. "Between you and Pastor Tim, how could a guy say no?"

"See you around two," I say as I get in my car and leave. Suddenly it feels like May 23 is just around the corner!

~*~

Of course, I get second thoughts about dinner with Noah once I'm home and have time to think about it further. Would Principal Marshfield consider my sharing a meal with Noah and his family to be breaking the rules? It's such a gray area, and I wish for the first time that Sofie had been placed in Cassie's class not mine. How much simpler it would have been! Noah and I could have started dating months ago.

Knowing that Ellie and Margaret will be there, it won't be like a *real date* with only Noah and me. Convincing myself that we're just bending—but not breaking—the rules, I get out my grandmother's biscuit recipe. There's nothing like Grandma

Bessie's warm biscuits slathered in butter. Grabbing flour and baking soda from the pantry, I put my worries aside and bake.

Noah's house smells delicious when I arrive. Ellie greets me at the front door, and we share a warm hug.

"Rae, it's so great to see you," Ellie says with a wink.

"Yes, especially since we just saw each other on Thursday," I tease. Ellie had picked Sofie up when a meeting with one of Noah's clients ran over.

"Um, those smell good." She nods towards the basket in my hands. I wrapped the biscuits in two towels and tucked them in the basket, hoping to keep them warm.

"My grandmother's biscuits," I say as I follow Ellie into the kitchen. "We might have to warm them up for a few minutes."

The kitchen is a hive of activity. Noah smiles and waves from his position at the counter carving the ham. Margaret gives me a quick hug as she flits by with a bubbling casserole dish and sets it on the dining table already set with plates and silverware. Sofie's folding festive-looking napkins and carefully placing them beside each plate.

"Can I do anything?" I say to the room.

"We're almost ready," Noah says as he lifts the platter of ham and carries it into the dining room.

"Let's pop those biscuits in the microwave for a few seconds," Ellie adds.

We heat the biscuits and Ellie finds a tub of margarine in the fridge. I should have brought real butter, but I didn't think of it.

Once we're all settled at the table, Margaret instructs us to join hands, then leads us in prayer. "Lord, thank you for bringing us together as family and friends today and thank you for this glorious meal. We are grateful for this time spent in fellowship together. In Jesus' name. Amen."

Amens echo around the table. Sofie's high-pitched voice joins in with the adult voices. I wink at Noah and he grins back.

Silverware clinks on the china plates, and our conversation is all about the food.

"The ham is cooked perfectly," I tease Noah.

He rolls his eyes. "It better be. This is my third ham, and now I'm a pro at fixing it."

"Unlike turkey," Ellie adds.

"Are these scalloped potatoes?" I direct the question to Ellie. "They're tasty and so cheesy."

Ellie laughs. "Actually, they're called 'Cheesy Potatoes.' I fix them for every holiday meal."

"It's the only kind she knows how to fix," Noah adds, and Ellie sticks her tongue out at him.

Margaret chuckles at the friendly banter as she butters her biscuit. "These are delicious, Rae. Did you make them from scratch?" she asks between bites.

I nod. "Grandmother's recipe."

Noah helps Sofie butter her biscuit, and she nibbles on it while ignoring her servings of ham, green beans, and potatoes. "Eat what's on your plate, Sofie," Noah says as he points his fork to the forlorn food. She wrinkles her nose but relents by taking a small bite of ham.

We talk about various topics. I describe how the sun shone through the stained-glass window at the sunrise service and what a magnificent sight it was. Once the plates are cleared, Margaret appears with her special cake displayed artfully on a crystal cake stand. A thick layer of coconut covers the icing, and on the top of the cake, the coconut forms what looks like a bird's nest. Three chocolate Easter eggs are nestled inside.

Sofie claps her hands while the rest of us "ooh" and "aah" over the cake. It is quite the creation and must have taken her several hours to prepare. Margaret cuts thick slices, which we adults enjoy with coffee while Sofie has her usual glass of chocolate milk.

"Wow Margaret, you really outdid yourself," Noah says as he leans back in his chair, patting his full stomach. Sofie gets into the act by patting her stomach as well, making everyone chuckle.

Noah and I clean up the kitchen, shooing Ellie and Margaret away. Sofie talks them into playing a rousing game of Candyland with her.

"Thanks for inviting me," I say as I load the dishwasher.

Noah's wiping down the counters and washing a few of the larger pots and pans. He looks at me over his shoulder. "I'm glad you came, Rae."

Our eyes lock and we exchange goofy grins for several long beats. He looks like he's going to kiss me, but a cheer from the dining room breaks the moment, and we return to our cleanup tasks.

As I prepare to leave, Noah walks me to the front door. He leans in and whispers, "May 23 is only thirty-five days away."

"Are you counting down the days?" I tease, knowing that I'm doing the same thing.

"Maybe?"

We exchange grins and I walk out the door.

Chapter Twenty-Six
Raelynn

MY BROWS KNIT WITH CONFUSION when I see the handwritten note on my desk on Monday morning. It's never a good thing when the principal calls you into her office.

"Knock knock," I say as I hover outside Principal Marshfield's office. My palms are sweaty, and my heart is beating at a faster rate than normal.

She looks up from her computer screen and smiles. "Come in, Rae. Close the door behind you, please."

It suddenly feels like a swarm of angry bees are attacking my stomach. I plaster a neutral expression on my face and take a seat across from the principal's desk.

She folds her hands on the top of the desk and looks me directly in the eye. I squirm internally at her fixed gaze. "Rae, I'm so pleased with your teaching. This being only your first year here, you are gelling with your colleagues, plus the kids and parents rave about you."

When she pauses for a few seconds, I feel there's a "but" coming. Concern and trepidation draw my eyebrows together and I pull in a big breath.

"Unfortunately, a parent has complained that you're seeing Noah Sullivan. The parent brought to my attention that you attended church service with Noah yesterday and that you two looked very 'cozy.' They're concerned that's a conflict of interest and that you will give his daughter preferential treatment. And, of course, you're already familiar with our school's 'no dating' policy." Principal Marshfield continues to stare intently at me, waiting for my response.

Nervously clearing my throat, I say, "Noah and his daughter attended church yesterday and they sat with me. He's going through a rough patch and I thought church would help him." The principal's expression doesn't change, so I continue. "Honestly, Mrs. Marshfield, I don't see how that breaks the rules. We're at church along with at least sixty other people."

She sits up straighter in her chair. "Rae, I'm sure that seems innocent to you, but I can't have my teachers giving any inappropriate impressions to other parents. Until the end of the school year I ask that you have no interactions with Mr. Sullivan outside of school when he drops off or picks up his child. I won't put you on probation, but this is a warning."

I furiously blink back tears, never intending to put my teaching career at stake. Unable to speak because of the emotion jamming my throat, I nod and stand.

Mrs. Marshfield puts up her hand, halting me from leaving. She gives me an encouraging smile. "I'm a firm believer that the best way to avoid gossip is to avoid any situation that can be misconstrued. It's really that simple."

"Thank you for the advice," I say stiffly, then walk out the door. My heart feels heavy as I make my way back to my classroom. I knew that Noah and I were stretching the rules a bit. Now, we have to the toe the line for thirty-four more days.

When my students start arriving, they lift my somber mood with their excited, happy voices. This is why I'm a teacher— molding and shaping these young lives. Purpose fills my heart, and I feel God gently guiding me. Noah and I can wait a month for our happily ever after.

Chapter Twenty-Seven
Noah

RAE CALLED ME IN TEARS because the principal gave her a warning about her relationship with me. A straitlaced parent saw us in church and complained. We've been mindful of that darn "no dating" rule the whole time, and I don't feel like we've broken it. But Rae said that her actions are under the microscope and that we can't do anything that could be "misconstrued" (Principal Marshfield's words, not mine).

For the first time, I wish that Sofie was in the other kindergarten class, but then would I ever have met Rae? I blow out a frustrated breath knowing that the next thirty-three days are going to be lonely. Rae says we can't have our nightly phone chats anymore either.

Maybe I need to take up a hobby to keep my mind off the beautiful teacher. Ellie's been bugging me to take Frankie to obedience classes. The dog can be naughty and hard of hearing at times. I investigate the schedule at the community center and sign up for an upcoming class.

Today's my day to visit all my clients. I make my rounds once a month and discuss any questions or changes in their business with them. It's an exhausting day, but I'm thankful for all my customers and this new job that allows me flexibility in my schedule. It has made a world of difference with meshing my schedule to Sofie's. A small frown crosses my face when I realize that the only time I'm going to see Rae in the next month is school drop off and pick up. We probably shouldn't even attend the same church service anymore—although I really need to continue attending because Pastor Tim's sermons are always uplifting.

Putting thoughts of Rae aside, I stride into Sacred Grounds for my meeting with Margaret. She's always the first client on my schedule because she insists on meeting me at the coffee shop so we can indulge in a sweet treat and a cup of coffee. Truth be told, me and my sweet tooth look forward to this meeting as much as she does.

Margaret's sitting at our usual booth in the corner. A carafe of coffee, two mugs, and a plate of blueberry scones sit on the tabletop. "Noah! Come sit down. I already ordered your favorite brew." Margaret holds up the carafe and waves it back and forth.

"You are sure chipper this morning, Margaret," I say as I slide into the booth while trying to stifle a yawn. "Sofie kept me up later than usual with an art project that was due today," I add as way of explanation for my sleepy state.

My client laughs. "What was it this time? A caterpillar made from an egg carton?"

"No, she already did that one," I say with a chuckle. "We were tracing and cutting out flowers on different colors of construction paper. The actual assembly of the project happens today at school. Frankly, I don't really know what the endgame is on this project."

A belly laugh floats across our section of the small café. "That's priceless, Noah," Margaret says as she wipes a few tears of laughter from the sides of her eyes.

I flip over one of the mugs and pour out a brimming cup, then grab a scone, letting the caffeine and sugar hit my system. We enjoy our food and drink in companionable silence until we polish off several scones and the carafe is empty. Margaret signals a waitress to come refill the carafe. "We can't have too much coffee," she says with a wink.

"What's new at Twice Again that I need to know about? Since we got you on QuickBooks, things have been running smoothly, right?"

Margaret agrees and then proceeds to tell me about a new section of the store that will sell handmade pieces made by local artists. We discuss how to set up a consignment arrangement with the artisans and what the profit splits should be. Ellie already told me about this new venture, and she's as excited about it as Margaret is.

Several minutes later, Margaret says, "Okay, Noah. No more shoptalk. Tell me what you have planned for that lovely teacher on May 23. How are you going to romance her?"

My eyes widen because I haven't talked to anyone about this except Ellie, who obviously told Margaret. *When will I learn that my sister can't keep her mouth shut?* "Um, well, I haven't thought about it too much yet."

A loud snort accompanies my words. "You have to plan ahead, Noah. I know a romantic restaurant in the foothills that's getting rave reviews. You should check it out online and make a reservation. I'll text you the name once I think of it."

I chuckle. "Thanks for the help, Margaret."

"Anytime, anytime." The glint in her eye tells me that she enjoys offering dating advice.

We wrap up the meeting and I feel a lightness in my step just thinking about how I'm going to "romance the beautiful kindergarten teacher" on May 23. Getting Margaret's help makes it easier; I just have to look up that place and get a reservation.

I walk three doors down from the café to the quilt store, which is quiet this early in the morning. Classes don't start until after noon, so I find Grace manning the register while working on a quilt.

"Good morning, Grace," I say to announce my presence since she's so absorbed in her work.

"Oh, Noah! I lost track of time. Let's go in the office for our meeting; I'll be able to watch for anyone who comes in."

174

I nod and follow her to the tiny office. "The quilt you were working on is beautiful. Are you going to sell it?"

She laughs. "No, I make every grandkid a quilt for their tenth birthday. This is my fifth one to make and I still have two to go."

"They must love them. Such a special gift."

She smiles. "It's my legacy to them. They can pass it down to their kids."

Nodding at Grace's loving gesture to her grandkids, I think about the feeling of family that permeates this small town. It makes me want even more to build a lasting relationship with Rae here in Paradise Springs. Marry her and have a couple more kids.

Grace and I review a couple of invoices from her vendors that had unexpectedly gone up this month. I make a note to contact the supplier to understand why. After I answer a few of her QuickBooks questions, Grace says, "Now tell me about your little romance with the kindergarten teacher."

My neck heats and my ears turn red. *Does everyone in this town know about Rae and me?* "Ah, well, there's not much to tell. We can't officially date until school is out since Sofie's in her class."

Grace shakes her gray head. "Principal Marshfield is so strict." She makes a *tsk tsk* sound and I don't know if that's approval or disapproval of the principal. "So, what's your big plan after the last day of school? Flowers? A romantic dinner?"

I open my mouth to respond, but Grace cuts me off. "Oh! I just heard about a wonderful new restaurant. They do that farm to table thing. I'll call my daughter and ask her for the name. You should definitely try it."

"Thank you, I appreciate the help, Grace."

She gives me a beaming smile. When a customer enters the store, I wrap up our meeting and let myself out. My shoulders shake with suppressed laughter. I'm two for two in terms of clients giving me dating advice. *I wonder who's next?*

After several more client meetings, I wrap up my day at Evans Garage. Fortunately, none of my other clients had dating advice, and I don't expect any from the taciturn garage owner either.

I walk into the busy service area looking for my client. He does a thriving business, that's for sure. Every bay is filled with a variety of vehicles, and mechanics scurry about wielding tools and making quite a bit of racket. A wrench falls onto the concrete floor with a loud *clang!* and the noise reverberates around the whole building. I finally spot Logan at one of the far service bays, bent over working on a motorcycle.

"Hey, Noah," he says as I approach. "I lost track of time working on this beauty."

The motorcycle looks to be a vintage one, but I'm clueless as to what makes it special in Logan's eyes. "Is now still a good time to meet?"

He stands, wiping his hands on a towel. "Yeah, let's go to my office."

We cram ourselves again into the tiny space that barely qualifies as an office. I shake my head in amusement at the piles of papers on his desk. He hasn't heeded my advice to go digital.

Logan hands me a box stuffed with papers and grins. "Here's last month's receipts."

At least I transitioned all his invoices from vendors to be online now, so the box is much less full than when I met with him the first time. "Thanks. Anything new we need to talk about? Have you thought any more about getting a cash register that could automate these receipts instead of continuing to use paper?"

We've had this conversation for the last eight meetings, so I don't expect a different answer, but I keep trying.

He grunts. "You don't give up, do you?" Beneath his gruff, bearded exterior there's a funny, engaging guy. You just have to dig for him.

I laugh and hold up a hand. "Fair enough. I won't mention it again."

A small smile tips his lips up. "I'm expanding to restore vintage vehicles. That motorcycle is our first client."

"Oh? That sounds interesting. Is there a lot of demand for that in this area?"

He nods while I take some notes on my iPad. "Ernie retired earlier this year, leaving vintage owners with no repair place. I decided to take on Ernie's old clientele. A few weeks ago, I met with Ernie's supplier of vintage parts, so we're set up to work on about anything now. Got a call about fixing a Model T last week, and that part is on order. I think this can be a lucrative addition to my business."

Nodding, I ask, "Do you plan on expanding the garage area as well?" I point towards the service bays already filled to capacity.

"Yep, Ernie offered to rent his old space to me. I might have two locations, one for vintage repairs and one for everything else."

"Give me the rent numbers and your fees for the vintage work and I'll do a revenue projection for you."

"You can do that?" His eyes go wide at my suggestion.

I laugh. "Yes, we want to make sure your new venture has a positive ROI."

Logan's eyes roll back in his head at my mention of anything having to do with finances. "Well, thanks. I'll get you those numbers next week."

I nod, knowing that the information will be scribbled on a slip of paper. Oh well. *You can lead a horse to water, but you can't make him drink.*

As I put away my tablet, Logan says, "So I heard you and the kindergarten teacher have a romance going on."

My mouth hangs open because that's the last thing I expected to come out of Logan's mouth. "We aren't officially dating until after school's out."

He laughs. "Mrs. Marshfield and her strict rules."

I wonder how he knows about that, but I don't ask.

"There's a new restaurant about twenty minutes away that all my customers rave about. Sounds like a romantic place with candles, white tablecloths, all that stuff. I'll ask my office manager and get you the name of the place."

"Thanks, I appreciate that." Logan doesn't look like he has a romantic bone in his body unless he's talking about cars. I hold back my laughter.

We finish our meeting and Logan returns to work on the motorcycle while I lug the box of papers out to my SUV. *How does everyone in this small town know so much about everyone else's business?* I'll have to tell Rae about all the romantic advice at our nightly call.

My heart sinks when I remember there's no more nightly calls. May 23 can't come soon enough.

Chapter Twenty-Eight
Raelynn

IT'S BEEN A COUPLE WEEKS since the warning from Principal Marshfield. Noah and I almost don't dare exchange more than two words when he's here with Sofie. Our interactions consist of a stilted "hello" or "goodbye" and that's about it. Since I put an end to our nightly chats, I don't even get to talk to him that way. Fortunately, Ellie, Margaret, and even Cassie keep me apprised as to everything Noah. I guess secondhand news is better than nothing. So far, his ex-wife hasn't reappeared. I'm sure it's just a matter of time until she does.

"I'm beat," Cassie says as she waltzes into my classroom and perches on the side of my desk.

"Me, too. Some days I feel like teaching these kids is like herding cats."

My friend roars out a laugh. "How true!" She leans in towards me and says in a low, conspiratorial voice, "I heard that Noah's planning to take you to a romantic restaurant on May 23. You better reserve the date."

"Oh? How did you hear this?"

She makes a zipping motion with her fingers beside her lips. "I'm sworn to secrecy. But it sounds like he's going to great lengths to woo you."

A giggle escapes. "Woo me? Are we in a historical romance novel now?"

Cassie blushes. "I may read a few too many of those," she admits.

Shaking my head in amusement, I say, "I don't have anything other than last day of school activities scheduled for May 23, so he can plan to his heart's content and I'll be there." This little tidbit will get back to Noah via whatever source is sharing information with Cassie—hopefully that's as good as me actually talking to the man himself.

"Principal Marshfield just sent out an email telling all the parents that the last day of school will adjourn at noon. You'll have the whole afternoon to get ready for your fancy date!"

My mind rifles through my paltry wardrobe, wondering what outfit is elegant enough for this occasion. My brow wrinkles when the only thing that comes to mind is a pink dress that I've worn several times to weddings.

"You don't have anything to wear, do you?" Cassie says.

"Am I that transparent?"

"Yep. But I'm here to help. Let's go shopping next weekend to find the perfect outfit." Cassie says with glee.

I sigh. Shopping isn't my favorite thing, but I could use Cassie's help. "Okay, but I have a firm budget and we can't exceed it."

Cassie grins. "Sure, of course."

Those warning words about my budget are brushed aside like a piece of lint by the look on Cassie's face.

~*~

Dress shopping is so stressful. The full-length mirrors reveal every flaw in my body, and I grimace at how the latest dress looks on me. Too full in the bodice and too tight in the waist.

"This one won't work at all. It doesn't fit," I say as I emerge from the dressing room to where Cassie's sitting.

She looks me over. "It would require some alterations."

I groan. "How about I just wear my pink go-to dress. It fits."

Cassie sighs. "You're ready to give up already? You've only tried on three dresses on so far."

I grimace. "Three dresses that don't fit and that look horrible on me," I remind my friend.

"I'm going to scour the racks one more time. Stay here," Cassie instructs as she trots off to the dress display area. I go back in the dressing room and take off the ill-fitting item.

"Try these two," Cassie says a few minutes later as she hands me two hangers over the top of the dressing room door. One dress is sky-blue and the other one yellow. "Spring colors, and both are the latest styles," Cassie adds.

"I'm not much of a fashionista," I grumble as I take the hangers from Cassie's hand. She laughs.

The light blue dress is beautiful. I run the silky fabric through my fingers. It slips over my head, and when I pull it over my hips, I'm pleased and surprised that the dress fits me to perfection. Staring at my reflection in the mirror I admit that this dress looks good on me.

When I peek out of the dressing room, Cassie turns to look at me. I walk into the hallway, modeling the dress for her. "Wow, Rae. You look gorgeous in that one! The blue is an ideal color for you. And the dress fits perfectly." She beams like a proud parent.

"I like it too." When I look at the price tag on the sleeve, my heart drops. "This one is too expensive."

Cassie whips open her purse and pulls out a coupon. "Will 25% off help?" she says with a grin.

I hug my sweet friend. "You're the best! Thank you."

All the while the sales lady rings up my purchase, I daydream about how much Noah will like the dress. It makes me feel confident and even a little sexy. I can't wait for May 23 so he can see it.

Chapter Twenty-Nine

Noah

VICKI CALLS THREE WEEKS AFTER she reneged on the visit to the zoo.

"Noah, I'm calling to see if I could take Sofie to the zoo this next weekend." She makes the offer without even apologizing for backing out the first time—or her radio silence since.

"I took Sofie to the zoo the weekend you backed out. She was so upset and was afraid she'd miss the baby hippos," I say in a cool voice.

There's a pregnant pause on the line. "I see. Well, thanks for doing that." Her voice is laced with sarcasm.

"Vicki, she's five and doesn't understand the concept of waiting a couple weeks. Plus, I wasn't sure how much I could trust you to follow through." My words come out harsher than I planned, but Vicki needs a wake-up call. Is she committed to visitations with our daughter for the long haul or only when it suits her?

She sighs. "I guess I deserve that. But you have to understand that my career comes first."

"That's crystal clear."

Another pregnant pause makes me wonder whether she hung up. "Noah, what do I have to do to get back into your good graces?"

Am I finally ready to forgive Vicki? Rae recently reminded me of one of Pastor Tim's sermons where he spoke about Joseph and how he forgave his brothers for selling him into slavery. I think it's time for me to trust in my faith and forgive my ex-wife once and for all.

I back off my inflexible stance, knowing that Sofie enjoys visits with her mom. "How about we work out a regular visitation schedule and you show me you can commit to it?"

"Thank you. This is unexpected." There's a sniffle on the other end of the line. "Would you agree to two Saturdays a month? I'll come to Paradise Springs until Sofie's comfortable coming to my house. With summer coming soon, Sofie and I should have all sorts of activities we can do together."

"What happens when your boss asks you to work again on a weekend?"

"Um, right. Maybe I should commit to only one Saturday a month and we leave it a little flexible? Just until I'm firmly established in my career."

I sigh internally when she mentions her career again, but she's being honest about it so that shows how much she's matured. "I'll have my attorney draw up the language and we can get the custody agreement changed to include one Saturday visitation a month." As soon as these words leave my mouth, I feel like a boulder has been lifted from my shoulders. *Forgiving Vicki is a freeing feeling.*

We talk about the wording that makes both of us comfortable. I let Vicki know that I'll call Jesper in the morning and ask him to make this modification.

"Noah, I really appreciate getting to see Sofie. You've done an exceptional job raising her. She's truly a joy to be around."

The unexpected praise from my ex-wife catches me off guard. "Thank you. I'll contact you once we have the modified custody agreement in place. Sofie's last day of school is May 23. I think she'd enjoy an outing with her mom that next Saturday."

"That sounds great! I'll reserve the date on my calendar." Vicki sounds excited and grateful. I'm cautiously optimistic.

After Vicki hangs up, I ponder how the situation with Vicki has taken a complete turn-around. When she reentered my life, I was at a low point, terrified of sharing my daughter with the mother who left us without a word. But I've come to realize that Vicki and I can share Sofie without losing something in the process. In fact, it's a win-win for the three of us. *Thank you, Lord, for helping me to forgive.*

When I pick up Sofie, I glance at Rae and automatically want to go over and tell her about the conversation with Vicki. But all I can do is smile and wave while Sofie collects her stuff, and we leave. I won't tell my daughter about the arrangement with her mother until everything's in place.

"Did you have fun at school today?"

Sofie excitedly tells me about the guest firefighter who visited. "His coat and pants were so big, Daddy! He said they protect him from a fire."

I smile and nod.

"Miss Dailey says we only have two weeks left until summer vacation. How many days is two weeks?"

Chuckling, I reply. "Fourteen days. Shall we count them down on the calendar?" I can get out the calendar I'm already keeping in my desk drawer and we can mark off the days together.

Sofie nods. "But I'm going to be sad not seeing Miss Dailey anymore. Can we invite her over sometimes?"

"That's a great idea. Maybe she can come over for lunch occasionally." I try not to laugh at my own little joke and hope that Rae will be coming over every day.

"Can we have grilled cheese and chocolate milk?"

A smile splits my face. "Of course." Apparently, all it takes to make my daughter happy is grilled cheese and chocolate milk.

Sofie sings to the radio and I bask in the confidence that Miss Dailey will be a part of our lives as soon as the school year ends. As it turns out, Margaret, Grace, and Logan all referred me to the same restaurant. After extensively researching the menu and reading the rave reviews online, I quickly made reservations for 7:00 on May 23. Fourteen days and counting!

~*~

I remind myself for the tenth time why I'm here surrounded by barking dogs and an instructor that looks like she could have been a drill sergeant in the military. Frankie needs to learn obedience, or at least how to take a walk without pulling on the leash all the time. A loud sigh escapes. *I'm an inept doggie dad and it shows.* My dog is one of the worst ones in the class. But hey, this is just the first night, so Frankie can only improve. *I hope.*

Clap! Clap!

Drill Sergeant Dottie looks sternly across all her class members, human and canine, with a scowl that would have Army recruits shaking in their boots. "Ladies and gentlemen, thank you for coming. By the looks of it, everyone here needs to learn discipline and who's top dog." A loud belly laugh escapes her ample chest while the class nervously snickers. "And let me tell you, your dog shouldn't be the one who's in charge." Her words sound similar to an episode of *Dog Whisperer* that I watched last week.

Frankie sits at my feet, vibrating with excess energy, ready to bolt across the gymnasium where the class is being held. She creeps forward on her stomach, slowly inching her way across the floor. I keep a tight hold on the leash and gently pull her back. Multiple times.

The dogs around us are also in various stages of misbehaving. A terrier yips nonstop, despite the owners feeble attempts at asking him to be quiet. A spotted dog that looks like a spaniel jumps up on his owner's legs. Every time the owner instructs the dog to lie back down, the dog sits then immediately jumps up

185

again. It reminds me of a poor comedy sketch repeating on a loop. A beautiful brindle colored behemoth lies quietly beside his owner, his head on his massive paws, and I think the Great Dane may have fallen asleep.

Dottie leads us through drills for teaching your dog to properly walk on a leash. After multiple circles around the gym, Frankie is not pulling quite as much. *Maybe all this peer pressure is good for her?*

We're given a sheet that details multiple obedience exercises Dottie wants us to do with our dogs during the week. These are the same exercises we did during class, so everyone is familiar with them. She calls it homework and encourages everyone to perform them at least twice a day. Repetition and reward are apparently the keys to successful dog training. I remind myself to pick up a bag of the recommended dog treats on the way home. Dottie swears by them.

By the end of the evening, I'm exhausted but feeling much better. Like a proud parent, my chest swells with pride that my dog did okay and didn't flunk out on the first night.

As I walk to the car, mingling and chatting with the other dog owners, a squirrel runs in front of us, immediately setting off a raucous round of barking from our pets. Frankie yanks on the leash, pulling it out of my hand. I stand forlornly as I watch her join a pack of five other dogs chasing after the squirrel. The animal runs several yards away and scampers up a tree, where our canines stand, barking and howling. One dog who looks like a coonhound is bellowing out an impressive baying sound that the breed is known for when they tree a raccoon. The mournful noise echoes around the neighborhood.

The coonhound owner looks at me and shrugs. "Guess Goofball has more to learn," he says with chagrin.

I shake my head in amusement and laugh. Guess all our dogs have more to learn. I'll diligently practice the obedience drills Dottie gave us for homework. My competitive nature wants Frankie to pass the class with flying colors. Plus I have the time until May 23rd.

Jogging over to the tree, I collect my naughty dog and head for home. *Maybe Sofie should bring Frankie next time.* Sadly, the dog obeys her better than me.

Chapter Thirty
Raelynn – May 23

MY THROAT FEELS SCRATCHY, my head throbs, and my nose runs like a leaky faucet. The sniffles and body aches I was feeling yesterday have accelerated into a full-blown cold. My heart and mood plummet knowing that I'm sick and I'll miss the last day of school. My heart sinks further knowing I'll also miss the romantic first date with Noah.

Painfully pulling myself out of bed, I drink some orange juice, hoping it will make me feel better. When a coughing fit racks my body, I know there's no hope that this illness is going away any time soon. Picking up my cell, I call Cassie.

"Hey Rae! Today's the day," she says in an excited voice.

I sneeze loudly. My voice comes out raspy and raw when I reply. "I'm sick, Cassie. That cold I was trying to ward off yesterday hit me full force this morning. I can't come in and expose the kids to this."

"Oh no!"

Blowing my nose, I sound like a wounded goose, and I apologize to my friend for the rude noise. "I'll call Principal Marshfield and hope a substitute can come in on such short notice."

"I can cover both classes if needed. Stay home and feel better." I hear a sound in the background that indicates Cassie is getting dressed while she talks to me.

"I really want to say goodbye to the kids. Could you set up a computer and video conference in my classroom so I can say goodbye to them?"

"That's a great idea, Rae. I'll get it all set up and call you when we're ready."

"Thanks for everything. You're such a wonderful friend."

We sign off and I call the principal. She tells me to get better and that she'll call Trudy, our usual kindergarten substitute. After I hang up, I want to cry in frustration. Not only is my last day of school a bust, but so is my date with Noah tonight. I was so looking forward to it! Realizing defeat, I text to let him know I'm sick and then return to bed until Cassie calls me about the video conference. *So much for the countdown calendar and my anticipation of May 23.*

~*~

The video conference is enjoyable despite how I feel. I shower and try to look better even though I blow my nose several times during the call. The kids crowd around the computer, waving and telling me to feel better. Trudy helped them make posters for me, and seeing their handiwork brings a tear to my eyes.

Before we sign off, each kid says something to the screen.

"My mommy was sick last week."

"Your nose is red. You look like a clown."

"Did you drink some orange juice?"

"Are you having chicken noodle soup? That makes you feel better."

"I don't like chicken noodle soup. It's yucky."

"No it isn't! Miss Jones, tell him that chicken noodle soup isn't yucky."

Trudy intervenes before there's a fight over chicken noodle soup. She wraps up the call and I tell the kids how much I'm going to miss them.

"Bye Miss Dailey!" they say in unison and everyone waves as we sign off.

I flop back down on my bed and promptly fall asleep.

~*~

189

Pound! Pound! Pound!

The noise rouses me from a restless sleep. Is that the pounding in my head or is someone at the door? I listen for a few seconds and realize that someone is at the door. *Who could it be?*

I trudge to the front door and open it a crack. Noah peers back at me. "Dr. Sullivan has come with soup and medication for the patient," he says in a breezy voice. I step back as he waltzes through the door.

I hold up a hand. "Don't get too close, Noah. I'm probably still contagious and I don't want you to get this."

He laughs. "I have an ironclad immune system. No worries." He strides into the kitchen carrying two paper bags. I follow him at a safe distance, hoping he won't pick up this bug. My kitten-adorned pajamas are wrinkled and I'm wearing fuzzy pink socks. My hair's sticking out at odd angles and a tissue sticks out of the pocket of my PJs. With my red nose and disheveled appearance, I'm surprised Noah doesn't turn around and run back out the door.

"Sit. You look like you're going to fall over." Noah points to one of the stools at my island, so I gratefully slump down onto it. I hold my head in my hands, hoping to lessen the throbbing. He starts taking stuff out of the bags and setting it on the countertop.

"Margaret sent her homemade chicken noodle soup," Noah says as he pulls out a large kettle from one of the bags. He sits it on the stove and turns on the burner. "It got a little cold on the way over because I stopped for these," he says as he reveals a package of saltine crackers, a two-liter bottle of 7UP, and a bag of chocolate kisses. "In case you feel like something sweet," he says with a wink.

My heart swoons at his thoughtfulness, although I think some of the items may be more appropriate for someone with a stomach bug, but I don't say anything. Once the soup starts bubbling on the stovetop, the aroma fills the kitchen and I smell the delectable odor despite my stuffy nose.

"Here's a Get Well card from Sofie. She came right home from school and made it for you."

I turn the sweet handmade card over in my hands. She used lots of her favorite crayon colors—turquoise and yellow. There's a bumblebee and flower drawn on the front. Tears spring to my eyes when I read the inside that she carefully wrote out in thick uneven crayon strokes to "M I S S ☐ A L Y." The backwards D makes me chuckle. "This is so sweet. Please tell her thank you," I say as tears leak out of the corner of my eye. Noah nods and continues to prepare lunch, putting out some crackers on a plate and, at my direction, getting out bowls for the soup.

Once the soup is dished up, Noah carries the bowls to the table, and we sit across from each other. This is the first time we've been alone since the ultimatum from Principal Marshfield. *How romantic. Wearing my wrinkled PJs, sipping soup, and nibbling on a few crackers. This is a far cry from the fancy dinner Noah had planned.* Trying to sound upbeat, I tease, "Shouldn't we be having chocolate milk?"

Noah howls with laughter. "Chocolate milk is the cure to everything, according to Sofie." Once he's gotten his mirth under control he says, "I heard you had a video conference with the kids. It was all Sofie could talk about on the drive home."

I sniffle. "Yeah, but I wanted to be there so badly. I really made a mess of things for the last day of school and our first official date tonight." My voice cracks and I blink back more tears. I pull the tissue out of my pocket and loudly blow my nose. The awkward noise from my nose and the comfy clothes I'm wearing are a far cry from the sexy siren image I was hoping to portray in my new dress tonight.

The wonderful guy sitting across from me doesn't seem phased by any of my inelegant sounds or my frumpy appearance. He gives me one of his heart-melting smiles and passes me the plate of crackers. "We can go to that restaurant any time."

"I'm sorry I ruined our date." My voice wobbles with disappointment.

Noah reaches across the table and takes my hand, squeezing it in his much larger palm. "As long as I'm here with you, that's what counts. And we don't have to worry about Principal Marshfield finding out," he says with a glint in his eye.

I return his smile. "Can we still go to that fancy restaurant sometime? I even bought a new dress for the occasion." I sigh loudly and my voice rings with disappointment.

Noah raises an eyebrow. "I can't wait to see you in that. As soon as you're feeling better, we'll reschedule."

Nodding, my heart beats faster in anticipation of the future date. I finish the delicious soup, not realizing how hungry I was. "Please tell Margaret this was yummy."

"If you give me a container, I'll leave the rest with you."

Noah finds a plastic container and puts away the leftovers in the fridge, then turns to leave.

"I appreciate you feeding me. I hope you don't get sick."

He laughs as if that isn't even remotely possible.

"Today was still special because of you, Noah."

"If you weren't contagious, I'd give you a kiss," he says with a gleam in his eye that causes my heart to do a flip.

Noah then walks out the door, leaving me speechless picturing that kiss. "I'll look forward to that," I say to the now-empty room.

After Noah's gone, I pull out my countdown calendar, adding a red X to May 23. I put away the calendar, snickering at how sometimes our best laid plans go astray. *God, thank you for bringing Noah and Sofie into my life. I truly am blessed.*

Chapter Thirty-One
Noah

AFTER RAE RECOVERED FROM HER ILLNESS, I caught it. So much for my ironclad immune system. It's been over two weeks, and we still haven't gone on the "official first date" yet. We laugh about it because we've gone out a couple times, just not alone, and not to the fancy restaurant. It's still on our list as soon as life slows down a little.

Since school let out, I've added five new clients and they're keeping me remarkably busy. Nothing like word of mouth to expand your client base. My new clientele consists of Margaret's friend who opened a bakery, Grace's cousin who sells handmade jewelry online and at Twice Again, Logan's best buddy who started a BBQ joint and root beer stand, the owner of the Cozy Inn B&B who knows Ellie, and Pastor Tim's brother who opened an organic food market on Main Street.

Today Rae, Ellie, Sofie, and I are enjoying lunch together at the new root beer stand. Ellie agreed to bring Sofie with her, so I could finally get a few minutes of alone time with Rae. I pick Rae up at her house, bustling inside when she answers the door.

I close the door behind me with an air of finality and gaze at this woman who has captured my heart and soul. My heart rate ticks up at what I plan to do in just a moment.

"Don't we have to leave?" she says with a puzzled expression. Even in a simple pair of shorts and a T-shirt, Rae's beauty dazzles me.

"Not before I do this," I say as I haul her into my arms, planting a firm kiss on her luscious lips which have been enticing me for months.

She sighs and eagerly returns the kiss. This first kiss is even more spectacular than I imagined. I've dreamt about kissing her since we met at the coffee shop to discuss the stained-glass window project. Always wondering if her lips are as soft as they look. . . They are.

Gently tugging her closer, I feel her body pressed against mine, it's as if we're made for each other. Since I've been longing to kiss her for almost six months, the kiss has a little more simmer than I originally planned. By the time we break apart, we're both a little breathless. *Wowza!*

"Oh my, that was worth waiting for," Rae says, as she waves a hand in front of her face, a blush highlighting her cheekbones.

"I couldn't wait any longer," I reply with a flirty grin.

Rae giggles. "Well, don't wait too long for the next one."

I laugh and pull her in for another quick kiss. Let's just say we were a few minutes late to the root beer stand.

~*~

The next morning, a squeal rings throughout the house. Sofie, with Frankie at her heels, runs into the kitchen where I'm enjoying a quiet cup of coffee.

"Today's my birthday!" she shouts.

I stand and pick her up, planting a sloppy kiss on her cheek. "Six years old," I say as she squirms excitedly, then I return her to her feet so she can dance around the kitchen singing the birthday song. I shake my head in disbelief—my little girl is growing up.

"When is the party?" she asks impatiently while she pours out a usually-banned sugary cereal consisting of multi-colored marshmallow shapes into her bowl. I relented and let her have it for her birthday. When I see the colorful hearts, stars, clovers, and rainbows in the bowl I question the wisdom of that decision. *Food isn't supposed to be pastel blue, green, and pink.*

The party timing question has been asked and answered at least twenty times this week. "Two o'clock this afternoon. It's nine now, so that's five hours away."

Her eyes grow big. "Can everyone have chocolate milk?"

Chuckling, I reply, "Yes, everyone can have some." I bought two gallons yesterday, which with any luck will be plenty.

"Is Mommy coming?"

I nod. "Yes, she'll be here." Probably not on time, but I'm confident she won't miss Sofie's special day.

Sofie bobs her head and happily shovels in spoonfuls of cereal, then slurps up the remaining milk in her bowl that has turned a pinkish color. *I'm going to quietly throw out the rest of that cereal.*

Just one year ago, Sofie's birthday party consisted of me and Ellie. Now we're having a cookout in the backyard and so many guests I've lost track. My life has changed so much in a year. *I'm enormously grateful.*

~*~

Rae arrives an hour before the party to help set up. I greet her at the front door, pulling her in for a quick kiss, which the birthday girl promptly interrupts. Rae winks and rubs her fingers on my cheek, mouthing "hello to you too" before we pull apart.

"Rae, Rae! It's my birthday!" As soon as the school year ended, Rae suggested that my daughter call her Rae rather than Miss Dailey and it stuck.

"A little bird told me that," Rae says.

Sofie stops hopping and draws her brows together. "A bird talked to you?"

Rae ruffles her hair. "It's an expression, silly girl."

Unphased, Sofie dances off into the kitchen, probably to find more sweet stuff to eat.

"How much sugar have you fed her?" Rae says with a smirk.

"The birthday girl can eat whatever she wants on her birthday. That's the rule."

Rae laughs. "The birthday girl's dad will regret that decision."

We set up the long folding tables I borrowed from the church in the backyard, along with folding chairs. When I invited Pastor Tim and his family to the party, he insisted on loaning me the tables. In fact, the man himself delivered them in his pickup truck. He's always ready to lend a hand.

"Did you finish the painting you were working on yesterday?"

Rae looks up at me from adjusting the legs on the table we're setting up. "I did and it turned out great. Margaret is going to feature it in the artisan gallery at the store."

My girlfriend has turned her artistic talent into a little side business since school let out. She's sold several paintings at Twice Again's new gallery. "I'm proud of you, sweetheart, you're so talented."

She blushes at my praise and my term of endearment. "My hobby is quickly turning into a business venture. I might need a certain accountant to help me," she says with a wink.

I walk over to her, enclosing her in a big bear hug. "As long as you pay in kisses, I'm here to help." Our lips meet for another kiss, and this time we're not interrupted. I lose track of time and focus only on the beautiful woman in my arms.

A noise from the neighbor's yard reminds us we're not alone. Rae giggles and playfully elbows me in the ribs. "Behave yourself, Noah Sullivan. Our guests will be arriving soon."

I love the way that she says "our." Rae's quickly fitting into our little family. She shares lunches and sometime dinners with Sofie and me, and we've begun our nightly chats again. It's such a relief not to have the "no dating" rule hanging over our heads anymore. We can do something as simple as going to the root beer stand without fear of repercussion.

Once the yard is ready, we go back into the kitchen and start the food prep. We're having the usual cookout fare of hamburgers and hotdogs. Ellie's bringing potato salad and Margaret insisted on bringing the cake. Rae's cutting up veggies and fruit for a healthy choice tray, and she's going to make a tossed salad.

A knock at the front door is followed by Ellie letting herself in, trailed by Margaret. "Hello! Where's the birthday girl?" Sofie runs into the front room and I hear her 'oohing' over the cake. When they all appear at the kitchen doorway, I see why Sofie exclaimed over the cake.

"Margaret, that's beautiful. How did you get it to look so much like Frankie?" Rae says as we both walk over to closer examine the cake. It's a perfect replica of Sofie's beloved pet—who barely graduated from the obedience class.

"Oh shoo! I took a cake decorating class one time and learned how to make these," Margaret says with pride in her voice.

"You should make these for parties and sell them. It's very professional," I add.

Margaret laughs. "I don't need another side business; this is just for fun."

Guests start arriving, so I hustle to get the grill going and the meat cooking. Rae directs the rest of the food prep and sets up the serving table with the condiments, chips, and salads. There's also a cooler stuffed full of sodas and bottled water sitting on a bed of ice. The gallon jug of chocolate milk will come out at the last minute. Sofie won't let us forget that.

When the first hamburgers and hotdogs are cooked, I call everyone over. "Thank you all for coming to help celebrate Sofie's sixth birthday." Guests clap and cheer while Sofie takes a bow. "Please serve yourself from the table and then come over and get a burger or dog, hot off the grill."

The crowd forms a line; happy conversations echo around me. I glance across our guests. Frank and June along with June's granddaughter . . . Riley who works at Twice Again, as well as her baby daughter . . . Cassie and her latest boyfriend. . . Pastor Tim, his wife, and two kids, his booming voice reverberating all around the yard . . . A couple of Sofie's kindergarten classmates, including Angela of crayon infamy. They're now best friends.

Kids squeal as they play on the playset I just installed in the backyard. It can be moved with us when we're done renting this house. Adults laugh and discuss the food. Being surrounded by all these friends makes my heart sing.

Vicki arrives fashionably late, as usual. Sofie runs to her side. "Mommy! Mommy!" Vicki bends down and I'm reminded at how much mother and daughter look alike. They have a conversation and Sofie nods her head a couple times.

Vicki asked me if we could split the cost of a new bike for Sofie, so we did that. The bright pink bike is hiding in the garage until after the party so we can give it to her in private. Since Sofie has so many toys, we asked that the guests not bring any presents but give a donation to a local charity instead. Sofie picked out the area women's shelter when I explained how kids who don't have dads sometimes have to go there without even their favorite toy. Sofie and I are going to visit there next week with any donations we receive in her birthday cards.

After everyone has gone through the line once, Pastor Tim comes over where I'm grilling the final round of hamburgers. "Noah, looks like you've settled into your new place very well."

I laugh. "It looks a lot better than it did on moving day, that's for sure." Turning serious, I add, "When I got fired, I thought my career was over. My life was in ruins. My faith was tested." He nods as I sweep my hand across the crowd. "Thankfully God put all these people in my path and I'm happier than I've ever been." *Thank you, God, for these unexpected blessings.*

The pastor smiles. "Sometimes God gives you a gentle push to put you on the right path."

I chuckle. "Well, getting fired wasn't exactly gentle. But it was a blessing in disguise, as they say."

Pastor Tim takes a sip from the can of soda in his hand. "Has your faith been restored?"

My brows draw together as I carefully ponder his words. "Yes. Restored and strengthened." *Just like the FaithBridge stained-glass window.*

"I suspect a certain kindergarten teacher had some influence," he says as he nods his head towards Rae. He winks, then walks away.

Glancing over at Rae, it hits me like a ton of bricks that she's the love of my life. *Now what am I going to do about it?*

Chapter Thirty-Two

Raelynn

AFTER TWO MONTHS OF DATING, we're finally going on our first "official date" tonight. Cassie teases me about what a slowpoke Noah's been at getting this rescheduled. I don't mind because just spending time with Noah and Sofie is better than five hundred fancy dates.

Noah arrives a few minutes early. I unlock the front door but remain hidden behind the closed door. "Come in but don't peek. I'm not quite ready yet." I run back off to the bedroom as I hear the door open and close.

"I'm not peeking," he yells.

Shaking my head at his teasing, I look in the mirror, swipe on some lip gloss, and grab my clutch purse. No oversized, chunky purse will do tonight. Checking to make sure I have everything; I emerge from the bedroom, saunter back to the living room, and strike a sexy pose.

Noah's sitting on the sofa looking down at his phone and doesn't even look up. *So much for my grand entrance.* I clear my throat and he finally looks up. His eyes widen and he stands. "You look stunning, Rae. That color brings out your eyes." He slowly walks towards me and grasps my hands. "Definitely worth the wait."

A warmth spreads up my neck and across my cheeks as I blush at his comment and his enthralled look. We gaze into each other's eyes for I don't know how long. He leans in and gives me a gentle kiss, the softness of his lips inviting me to return it with a soft sigh. I lose track of time, but finally come out of my haze when my stomach reminds me that I'm hungry.

Hoping Noah didn't hear the inelegant noise, I say, "You clean up nicely, Noah Sullivan." He looks so handsome in his suit, and he's wearing a blue tie that almost matches my dress. I suspect he had help from either Cassie or Ellie picking that out.

"Shall we go?" he says and whisks me off to his luxury SUV. I'm secretly glad that he didn't have to give up this vehicle when he had the financial crisis last year.

The drive to the restaurant is a blur. I can't get my mind off the hunky guy sitting next to me. We've come a long way since that awkward beginning almost a year ago when I handed him that write-up slip for Sofie. At least we moved on from that inauspicious start.

It's a Friday night, and the restaurant is crowded with people lining the walls of the waiting area, talking in small groups or sipping on a drink. I'm thankful Noah made a reservation because I'm not looking forward to standing in these high heels for any length of time. The hostess grabs two menus and seats us as soon as Noah gives her his name.

"This place is fancy," I say with awe lacing my voice as I glance around the room. Two-person tables are spaced a tasteful distance apart, giving each couple privacy. Pristine white tablecloths adorn the tables, along with a single lit candle that flickers, providing a classy, romantic vibe.

"My extensive research and all of my sources said this was the place to take someone special."

I giggle at the typical Noah comment. "Who were your sources?"

He winks. "I'll never tell."

The waiter returns and we place our orders. I order a fish dish whose name I can't pronounce. The waiter assures me it's baked halibut on rice. Noah orders steak. Once it's just the two of us again, Noah reaches across the table and takes my hand. "I'm sorry it took me so long to get this rescheduled."

"Since I was the one who made us miss the first time, I can hardly complain."

Everything fades into the background as we hold hands, letting our eyes carry on the conversation. My heart thumps in my chest at Noah's soul-searching gaze. He makes my knees weak, and the room feels several degrees warmer than when we arrived. When the waiter appears with our entrees, we reluctantly pull our hands apart.

Each plate looks as though the food is arranged for a gourmet cuisine photoshoot. Noah leans towards me and says under his breath, "Should we eat this or just take pictures?"

I giggle. "Take one picture and then we'll eat." He takes several shots on his phone. "Share those with me after we're done." He nods.

Although the portions look small, the food is rich and delicious. I'm full before we get to the dessert course, so Noah and I split a slice of decadent chocolate cake. Of course, it has some fancy name other than *chocolate cake.*

The waiter clears out our plates and brings two flutes filled with champagne, the bubbles playfully rising in each glass. I raise an eyebrow when these appear. "Did you order these?" I whisper after the waiter is out of sight.

Noah gives me his knee-weakening smile and pulls a small box out of his suit pocket.

My heart skips a beat.

"Rae, you're the light of my life. I love you and want to spend the rest of my life with you. Will you marry me?"

I gasp and put my fingers up to my mouth when he flips the box open. My heart races as I look at the gorgeous ring. Holding out a finger for Noah to place the ring on, my hands shake while tremors run through my body.

"Is that a yes?" he says, sliding the ring on my trembling finger with a chuckle.

A tear slides down my cheek as I stare in shock at the beautiful diamond. "It's definitely a yes!"

The waiter comes back and offers to take our picture, which we gladly allow him to do. Couples around us say "Congratulations" as we finish the champagne.

"I thought about hiding the ring in the dessert or the champagne, but you always see how badly that ends in a movie—the woman swallows the ring and has to go to the hospital. So, I went the more conservative route," Noah explains.

"This is perfect." My voice comes out barely above a whisper because emotion blocks my throat.

"When should we tell Sofie?" Noah asks.

Since it's already past her bedtime, I don't want to wake her up tonight. "How about we all go out for pancakes tomorrow and we tell her then?"

Noah smiles. "Sounds perfect. She's going to be so excited."

"And we'll all have chocolate milk," I add, which causes both of us to laugh.

I gaze at the man I love with all my heart, my eyes still filled with tears of joy. "I love you, Noah Sullivan, and I can't wait to be your wife."

He nods, staring back at me with love shining in his eyes. Several minutes later we walk hand in hand out of the restaurant. I'm happy and content knowing Noah's love for me won't be shattered by any future bumps in the road. Our faith in God and our love for each other will get us through anything.

THE END

Note to Readers

Dear Reader—thank you for reading Book 6 in the Potter's House (Three) series. I am honored to be part of this wonderfully inspirational series of clean Christian romances.

I hope Rae and Noah's story brought you many hours of happiness, some laughs, and maybe a few tears. Watch for Riley and Logan's story, **A Reason for Hope**, Potter's House (Three) Book 13, November 2021.

I always put a tidbit from my own life into my books. The scene where Noah takes Frankie to doggie obedience school was inspired by my own experience taking our Brittany Goldie to obedience school. Let's just say Goldie wasn't the best student in the class either.

I've always admired stained-glass although I'm not an expert in its repair and restoration. I used this website as a reference and based much of what Noah, Rae, June, and Frank did for the church windows on this article: Old Leaded Glass: repair, restore or replace?

An author's most gratifying reward for all our hard work is that you enjoy one of our books and find inspiration in the story. Let me know if that's the case! I love hearing from my readers—Email me at leahb1959@gmail.com.

Also, please take a moment to leave a review on Amazon. Just a few words can inspire another reader to take a chance on this book.

Please follow me on my website, Facebook, or Amazon author page or subscribe to my newsletter to be informed about upcoming book releases, sales, and special promotions. Links to all of those are included in the "<u>About the Author</u>" chapter below.

Thank You and Happy Reading.

Acknowledgements

Thank you to my amazing editor Bonnie McKnight. She's been with me every step of the way. Her suggestions and encouraging comments improved this story. She makes me a better writer and I truly appreciate her wisdom and guidance.

I'm thankful for all the wonderful people in my life. A little piece of each of you finds its way into my stories. And I'm especially grateful to my supportive husband who chuckles when he sees himself in one of my books.

We're blessed to live in Colorado, whose magnificent landscapes are the inspiration for my descriptions of Paradise Springs. The snow-capped mountains, green valleys, and clear blue skies are a stunning example of God's handiwork.

Of special note: I took the snow-capped mountain photo gracing the cover of this book. Thanks to Delia for incorporating it into her gorgeous cover design.

About the Author

Leah Busboom wanted to become an author since the day she learned how to read. She specializes in the Romance genre because she loves a sweet romance with a happy ending. Her books are known for their heartwarming stories; intriguing characters and hilarious real-life situations that will make you want to laugh out loud.

Leah currently lives in Colorado with her wonderful husband, her "Blue Bomber" bicycle and a hundred bunny rabbits that roam free in the neighborhood.

Find out about Leah's latest book releases, sales, and giveaways:

- AuthorLeahBusboom.com
- Newsletter Sign-up and access to bonus Epilogue
- Leah Busboom Facebook Author Page
- Amazon Author Page

Books by Leah Busboom: (all available on Amazon)

The Potter's House (Three) series: (Christian romance)

- *A Time for Faith* – Rae & Noah's story (Book 6)
- *A Reason for Hope* – Riley & Logan's story (Book 13) – Coming November 2021

Connor Brothers Series: (Clean & wholesome romance)

Can't get enough of the Connors? Here's the complete series so far:

- *Finding You*—Hailey and Quinn's story (Book 1)
- *Loving You*—Maddie and Max's story (Book 2)
- *Wanting You*—Daisy and Jacob's story (Book 3)
- *Needing You*—Ashleigh and Brock's story (Book 4)

- *Mistletoe, Tinsel & You*—Sylvie and Ford's story (A Christmas Novella, Book 5)
- *Casseroles, Kisses & You*—Bea and Nate's story (A Valentine's Novella, Book 6)
- *Rescue Me*—Starr and Bryce's story (Book 7)
- *Inspire Me*—Addison and Ian's story (Book 8)
- *Choose Me*—Luci and Austin's story (Book 9)
- *Return to Me* – Mary Sue and Cooper's story (Book 10)
- *The Holly Berry Dress & You* – Amelia and Doug's story (A Holiday Novella, Book 11)

Chance on Love Series Trilogy: (all available on Amazon.com)

- *Second Chances*—Matt and Samantha's story (Book 1)
- *Taking Chances*—Danny and Paige's story (Book 2) (Winner: 2018 Rocky Mountain Cover Art Contest—Sweetest Cover)
- *Lasting Chances*—Gabe and Megan's story (Book 3)
- Chance on Love Series Boxed Set – Books 1-3 in Chance on Love series

Unlikely Catches Series Trilogy:

- *Catching Cash's Heart*—Holly and Cash's story (Angel Wings & Fastballs) (Book 1)
- *Stealing Alan's Heart*—Brianna and Alan's story (Stilettos & Spreadsheets) (Book 2)
- *Winning Trey's Heart*—Abby and Trey's story (Playboy & the Bookworm) (Book 3)
- *Unwrapping Sam's Heart* – Lynn and Sam's story (A Christmas Novella) (Prequel to Book 1)

- *Melting Nick's Heart* – Bethany and Nick's story (A Valentine's Day Novella) (Sequel to Book 3)

Made in United States
Orlando, FL
22 July 2023

35381234R00115